A Man for the Country

A Man for the Country

By

Dave P. Fisher

First Edition

Printed in the United States of America and Australia.

Bottom of the Hill Publishing
Memphis, TN
www.BottomoftheHillPublishing.com

ISBN: 978-1-61203-470-6

10 9 8 7 6 5 4 3 2 1

Cover Art

Mountain Road

By

Joe Sambataro

Master artist Joe Sambataro was born in Philadelphia and is a scholarship graduate from the famous Layton School of Art. He has a B.F.A. degree through Marquette University/Wisconsin Medical College, Milwaukee Area Technical College and Masters Degree studies through the University of Wisconsin.

A consistent award-winning artist, Joe Sambataro has earned popularity worldwide. He resides and maintains a studio in Texas, and his paintings are widely sought after by corporations, government agencies and private collectors. You are invited to view Joe's magnificent artwork by visiting www.SambataroStudios.com.

While visiting Joe's website, check out his autobiography entitled PAINTING WITHOUT NUMBERS. The book is a great read, and is available through Joe at his website.

Joe says, "I am so lucky to be doing what I love. Art is not only a form of communication but also an expression of yourself. I realize what a great privilege it is to share that with others and I am thankful every day."

Bottom of the Hill Publishing is proud to feature the artistry of Joe Sambataro on the cover of this book.

www.SambataroStudios.com

Table of Contents

Chapter 1

The wall that separated the Drewsey Café from the adjoining saloon was paper thin, thin enough to hear every word spoken behind it. Devon McCloud froze in place, holding a forkful of potatoes mid-way between the plate and his mouth. He had been trying to hold a conversation with his wife seated across the table from him, but the loud voices from the saloon made it a futile effort. It was beginning to grind on his nerves, when he heard the name 'Richards' spoke in an angry tone.

With his fork poised in front of him his eyes met Katy's, they both shared the same question. Slowly he lowered the fork and strained his ears to try and pick up the rest of the saloon talk. At the same time he and Katy turned their eyes to the wall as if expecting to see through it.

A full year had passed since the last shot was fired at the Chaney ranch house by Charles Sampson's hired guns. It had been a peaceful and productive year, with the Bitter Grass seeing more success than it had seen in the previous five. They had received a letter from Marshal Vaughn, in Baker City, that Charlie Sampson had been sentenced to ten years in the state prison for his part in what had come to be known on the high desert as the 'Bitter Grass War.' Sampson's sentencing put what they thought was a capstone on the range war that had almost destroyed them.

The story of how three men, a woman, and an old lady had held off everything Charlie Sampson and Egg Taylor could throw at them spread like wildfire. It was the topic of conversation in every saloon and cow camp from the Wallowas to Jordon Valley, and even over into Idaho. Sampson was not well liked by most men in the area and his downfall was met with laughs and affirmations to the fact that justice had been served.

Not too much was said as to Brian Richards buying the Wire Creek out from under Sampson. Most folks didn't care that he was from England and owned one of the biggest cattle operations in the state. However, Sampson did have his supporters, or at least those who sided with him strictly because he was "one of us." It was anticipated that there would be some ill-will directed towards

Richards.

The expected grumblings among the local ranchers had begun a month back. Devon had heard the first of it when he brought a dozen head of steers into the Drewsey pens to sell. At first it was nothing worth paying much attention to, just some locals complaining about the Englishman controlling such a large amount of country. He had actually laughed it off when he heard one man make the statement that the Queen of England was going to come and take Oregon back and use Richards to do it.

The talk grew from ridiculous off-hand comments to dangerously serious. The day he heard a man curse Brian Richards' name and say that "they needed to run him out," was the day he stopped laughing it off. Now Brian's name was up again in the saloon next door. He decided that he had had enough of the bad-mouthing his friend was receiving.

The voice came again, "Yeah, that Richards stole Chuck's ranch, just took it right out from under him, and then had him arrested to boot!"

A second voice, with a drunken slur to it, rose above the first speaker. "He stole it alright ... him and that no-account McCloud. Damn liars the whole lot of 'em, claiming Chuck shot up their place and all – it never happened."

"Yeah, a pack of lies to steal ol' Chuck's place. I say we burn him out and run his tail back to England. Do it for Chuck."

"And he can take that Devon McCloud with him too."

The first voice laughed low and dirty, "Leave that woman of his though, I'd like to have her."

Katy McCloud turned her eyes back to her husband.

Devon's face was growing dark as he calmly stood up and dropped the checkered cloth napkin on his plate of half-eaten dinner.

Katy reached out her hand and placed it on Devon's arm. "Let it go Devon, they're drunk."

"A drunken man's words are a sober man's thoughts." He continued to move away from the table.

Katy knew all to well what was going on in her husband's mind. Once he set himself on a course of action there was no stopping him, he intended to take care of business. Be it a man or bronc, when Devon McCloud's face turned dark and his jaw clenched, nothing could turn him aside. He was going next door and she was powerless to stop him.

Without looking at Katy, Devon crossed the cafe and disappeared out the door. She followed him, but stopped when Devon grabbed ahold of the doorknob on the saloon door and slammed it back against the wall.

Stepping just inside the doorway, Devon studied the room and each man in it. There was a dozen men scattered throughout, but only two at the bar, both were half-way to drunk. There wasn't a man in the room that hadn't heard of the war between the Chaneys and Charlie Sampson. Sampson had no friends in the room, just those who intended to claim him as one in order to have an excuse to make trouble for Brian Richards. The two standing at the bar were among those.

Brian Richards was still a subject of study in the region regarding whether or not he belonged in the high desert, if he was a man fit for the country. His ranch manager, Sam Raven, was well liked and had a solid reputation, the fact that he rode for Richards was enough to convince most of the men that Richards was acceptable.

Devon McCloud was another matter; little was known about him except that he was double-tough, hell on wheels with any kind of a gun, and a friend of the Englishman. That combination was enough. It was understood that to attack Richards was to attack McCloud and few men were as dangerous. Nobody wanted a piece of Devon McCloud.

The room went deathly silent as all attention turned to the man in the doorway. Everyone had heard the drunken ramblings of the two men, but had ignored them. The look on McCloud's face said that he had heard it as well and had no intention of ignoring it.

Devon recognized one of the drunks as Chic Took, a small-time rancher with a haywire outfit amounting to nothing; the other was Farley Knolls, part-time outlaw and full-time fool. Knolls had been hired once by Sampson to attack the Chaneys, but had been run off the place at gunpoint. He had no liking for either man.

The two men had enough liquor in them to loosen their tongues, but not so much that they didn't recognize what kind of corner they had painted themselves into. They held their places at the bar, not daring to move in fear that McCloud might think they were going for their guns. Their eyes widened as Devon locked his anger-filled eyes on them.

Moving with deliberate long strides, he quickly covered the space between them. While still moving, Devon came up with a hard right fist and drove it into Chic Took's face. With a cry of pain the man covered his face with both hands, but it wasn't enough to stop the blood from flowing between his fingers and dripping on the floor. Devon hit him again on top of his hands, dropping Took to his knees. Roughly grabbing the back of the man's collar, he dragged him across the room and flung him out the open doorway. He landed with a dusty thud in front of Katy. She managed to jump back just in time to avoid having him fall into her. Rolling in the dirt, Took moaned as he continued to keep his hands tight against his face.

Devon turned back into the saloon and slammed the door shut behind him. Farley Knolls was sweating and fighting his fear as Devon came back after him. Out of sheer reflex Knolls dropped his hand down on his gun butt and began to pull the .45 from the holster buckled around his waist.

Devon was six feet from him when he saw the gun coming out of Knolls' holster. Swinging his hand down, he came up with his Colt and stuck the bore two feet from the drunken man's face. The cocking hammer rang out in the quiet room like a blacksmith's hammer on an anvil. Time stood still for everyone in the room, especially Farley Knolls.

Knolls' arm refused to bring the gun up, as it hung there in his limp fingers. He knew his life was hanging by a very fine thread; he also knew Devon McCloud had no reservations about shooting him. He just stood perfectly still.

Devon growled over his outstretched arm, "Do it. Bring that gun up and let me blow your head off."

The man managed to move his fingers enough to let the gun drop to the floor with a hard thud. Devon held his position, the Colt unwavering.

"You the one who's going to burn Brian Richards out, or are you the fool that's going to take my wife?"

Farley Knolls' breath came in labored gasps. Pointing a weak finger at the door he whispered, "He said both of those things."

"Liar," Devon's statement was cold and flat. "That walls' pretty thin, I heard two voices and you said one of those things. Which thing did you say?"

The man nervously licked his lips, he had made the remark about McCloud's wife and Took had made the threat against the

Englishman. He knew McCloud was expecting an answer and admitting to the crude comment about his wife would get him shot. In this country a remark like that carried a death sentence and no one would fault McCloud for killing him. It was safer to admit threatening the Englishman.

In a stammering voice he managed to say, "I said that about the Englishman ... and I apologize for it. It was the whiskey talking."

Looking down the barrel of the Colt, Devon considered Knolls' admission. He knew the man was lying out of fear, he wanted to shoot him, but he had to accept it or be branded a murderer. Lowering the Colt, he let the hammer down and held the man's eyes in his cold deadly glare. "Brian Richards is my friend – my *very good* friend. Any man who thinks he's going to burn him out will have me and a few others to deal with."

Turning his head, he cast his gaze around at the other men in the room. "The rest of you can take that home with you, too. Leave Brian Richards alone."

With another silent glance around the room, Devon backed toward the door. Reaching the door, he pointed his right forefinger at Knolls. "You've had your warning. Next time I see you, you had better be cutting a trail away from me in a big hurry. I know you made the remark about my wife and I won't be forgetting it."

Opening the door, Devon walked back out into the sunlight. Turning, he looked at Katy. "We'd better go see Brian, there's going to be trouble. I'll tell you about it while we ride."

Pulling the black mare's reins loose from the hitch rail he mounted, while Katy toed the stirrup and swung up on her big bay. As they headed southwest toward Brian Richard's ranch, the men in the saloon were loosening back up.

Laughter began to make the rounds at Farley Knolls' expense. His constant boasting and big talk had earned him the disdain of most of the men in the area. He had touted himself as being a *bad man* and a gunfighter to be reckoned with. His being backed down was a show enjoyed by all. A puncher at a table let out a loud laugh, "Hey Farley, you need to go change your drawers?"

The rest of the room exploded in laughter. Knolls' face turned a dark crimson as he downed two more drinks in rapid succession. He would never live this down unless he killed McCloud, but he knew he didn't have the guts for it. Yet, if the others were willing to stick together like they had been talking about, they could all do it.

Picking up his gun and stumbling back from the bar, he made his way toward the door. A voice called out behind him, "Tell your pals that if they plan to run that Englishman out they'd better be ready to take on McCloud, that whole Juniper crew, and probably Trig Parker too. If you were smart you'd just leave that whole outfit alone."

Knolls turned and glared back at the men in the room. His eyes were glassy and wandering as he tried to intimidate them with his best badman look. His drunken expression was more comical than frightening, especially to the hard men who were laughing at him. He strained to come up with a tough remark for them but his humiliation was too much. Turning around clumsily he caught his boot toe on the leg of a chair and stumbled but grabbed the table before he fell. Finally, he managed to make his way to the door and stepped out into the light and silence away from the taunts and laughter.

Blinking, he pulled his hat down over his eyes to shield them from the light. He found Chic Took sitting in the dirt with his back against the saloon wall. "Chic, you okay?"

"No."

"Let's go find Mel and get him to do more than talk. It's time for some action and I want to see to it that McCloud pays for this."

Took's face was covered in dried blood and dirt, rolling his head against the wall he spoke low. "You go find him, I ain't feelin' so good."

Squinting his eyes against the glare, Knolls looked up and down the street, then suddenly stopped and stared at a man coming out of the General Store. "Never mind Chic, I just found him."

Turning awkwardly around, Knolls staggered his way toward the store and the man he wanted. "Mel, hold up there a minute."

Mel Johns watched as Knolls came toward him. "What do you want, Farley?"

"I want you to come over here and take a look at Chic Took, that's what I want."

Johns moved his head from side to side trying to pick him out and then he saw Took where he had been sitting when Knolls left him. "What's wrong with Chic?"

"That Devon McCloud beat 'em good... that's what."

"Why?"

"Because he spoke his mind about that Englishman Richards. McCloud heard it and let him have it. I was going to shoot him, but he got his gun on me and I couldn't. It's time for you to get the boys together and go after that thieving foreigner."

"I don't know Farley, I'm not sure if we're right about this. We really don't know what actually happened with Chuck Sampson."

"What? I was there with Chuck, I know what happened. Now, *you* need to do something about it."

Mel Johns nervously rubbed the back of his neck. "I wish that fellow that was here talking about it last month was here now. He seemed to know what was going on."

Knolls glared at Johns, "I don't know anything about that...I wasn't here with you. What I do know is that you were talking it up about running Richards off Chuck's place. Were you serious or just making noise?"

"No, I think we need to do something."

Knolls took a hold of Johns' sleeve and snarled in his face. "Then you'd better get to it or answer to me. I want McCloud to pay for what he did to Chic."

Mel Johns' cringed at the liquor smell on Knolls' breath as he was trying to think through the problem and not make Farley Knolls mad. "Okay Farley, I'll do something."

Letting go of Johns' sleeve Knolls smiled, "That's good, Mel. You get the men together at your place and we'll work out a plan to run that Englishman Richards all the way back to England."

"It'll take a couple of days to reach all the boys, but I'll do it."

Farley Knolls continued to smile; he would have his revenge on Richards and McCloud both and not even have to do it himself. He liked the idea, they'd be dead and if the law got involved Johns could take the rope. It was a good plan, but he wasn't sure who this stranger was that Johns was talking about. Why would some stranger want to run Richards out, what did he want out of this? He had a good reason to hate Richards and didn't want his plan ruined by some outsider horning in on his play. If need be he might kill this stranger too, right along with Richards and McCloud.

Chapter 2

The setting sun turned the sky a brilliant fire orange and cast the land in long shadows. A cool breeze eased the July heat and made the lodgepole and juniper sway with a soothing rustle of boughs. Devon and Katy pulled their horses up on a hill and gazed out over the land. Below them spread what used to be Charlie Sampson's Wire Creek ranch, it was now part of the Juniper Cattle Company and anything that had ties to Sampson was gone. The only exceptions were the cattle that still wore the WC brand and in time they would be gone as well, and only the Triangle J Juniper brand of Brian Richards would be seen.

Immediately after Richards had taken over ownership of the Wire Creek and everything on it, he began to take steps to improve the range. The cattle had been moved off entirely. Consideration was given as to how many additional animals the Bitter Grass and the original Juniper could hold, the appropriate number was moved to each, the remainder were sold off.

He then hired a crew of men to dig ditches from the river, across the sagebrush flats and into pot holes. The result was that the ponds and ditches filled with water after the thaw and spring rains came. Even now, in mid-summer, the land was still showing green and fresh in the fading light with pools of water reflecting the orange of the sky.

Richards had moved into Sampson's old house. He had thrown out everything of Sampson's, from the curtains to the furniture, and Sampson's personal belongings, and burned them. A thorough cleaning was given to the house, inside and out, and his furniture and property moved in.

He had then sent for Henry Holden to come over from England. Henry had been Richards' houseman for over twenty years and was taking care of finalizing business at the old place in London at the same time it was being sold. All of Brian Richards' business operations were now based out of his home in Oregon.

Henry also served as a cook when Richards was tied to the house on business, but most of the time he ate with his men in the chuckhouse. He had managed to bring back most of Sampson's old hands, men who knew the ranch, and brought in a first-rate hotel cook from Sacramento. A job on the Juniper was a prize to be won and every cowpuncher in three states wanted to get on.

Memories flooded through Devon's mind as he looked over the ranch. A thin trail of smoke coming from the chimney of the chuckhouse beckoned them on. He recalled the tension of the day they had ridden up to Sampson's front porch. The gunfire from Sampson's hired guns was still ringing in their ears as they sat horseback and watched Brian and Marshal Willard Vaughn step up on his porch and knock on the door. There was the satisfaction of seeing Brian pull the bank note out of his pocket and tell Sampson he was through. Then there came the relief of watching the Marshal lead him off in irons.

The house was now a place of welcome and he and Katy had spent many warm evenings in Brian's company. They had even braved the cold and came down with Abby to spend Christmas together with Brian and Henry. He smiled at the recollection when he heard that Brian had given each of his hands a month's wages for a Christmas gift to show his appreciation for all their hard work. Saying that the men who rode for him would die in his defense was an understatement.

The warm feelings Devon felt looking down on the house were chilled as he considered the purpose for their visit. The ominous mood against Brian that was spreading across the range was certain to bring their peace to an end. He knew there was another battle brewing and the ill feelings toward Brian were being festered by a handful of jealous men. They were poisoning the minds of anyone who would listen, creating a false case that Brian was a foreigner and didn't belong here. The mood was being fueled by someone and it needed to be stopped.

Nudging their horses forward, Devon and Katy made their way down the hill toward the house. The first lamp had just been lit and offered a glow out the front window as they stepped off their horses and walked up on the porch. Knocking lightly, they waited only a moment before the door swung open and a neatly dressed man looked at them.

The man's face broke into a broad smile, "Mister and Mrs. McCloud, how good to see you!"

Devon grinned in appreciation of the man's proper British accent in the midst of cattle country. "Henry, how many times have I told you not to call me Mister McCloud?"

Henry's smile remained and he chuckled, "Of course ... Devon." He then bowed slightly toward Katy, "Mrs. McCloud."

In a mock threatening tone Katy lowered her head and peered upward at him, "Henry ..."

Shaking his head he bowed again, "My apologies ... Katy."

"That's better. You'll just have to get used to how informal we are out here Henry, now relax, it's only us."

With another laugh Henry stepped aside, "I will try, but you have to remember I have been with Lord Richards for many years and in Britain we have certain customs we must follow. My father was the gentleman's gentleman for Lord Richards' father, and he would never approve ... but I will try."

Katy patted him on the arm, "You'll do just fine."

As the three were laughing together, Brian came out of the adjoining room. He was shuffling through a handful of papers when he looked up and saw his friends. With a warm smile he looked at each of them, "Have you two been teasing Henry about his very British ways?"

"Just reminding Henry he doesn't have to be so formal with us," Devon smiled toward Henry.

Richards handed the papers to Henry, "Henry, please file these for me and then bring something to drink for the McClouds."

Taking the papers from him, Henry nodded an acknowledgement and left the room.

Turning his attention to Devon and Katy, Richards directed them to have a seat as he settled back in a large leather chair. "Have you seen how well the range is coming along?"

Devon nodded, "We were looking it over as we rode down into it, and those ditches have really made the difference in greening up the country."

"I expect to be moving some of the cattle back over from the original ranch by the end of summer. Bill has done a grand job of bringing this part of the ranch up. When we start full operation, I will have him managing the entire eastern half and Sam will continue managing the western. How are conditions fairing on your ranch?"

"Good. We had a pretty decent calving season. Creeks are still flowing and we've even sold off most of the steers for some operating money."

Richards nodded, "Excellent. And how is Abby? I haven't seen her in months."

Devon laughed, "As ornery and full of vinegar as ever."

"I can picture her as being just that way. And the Parker boys, how are they doing?"

"I was over to their place a few days back," Devon stopped and laughed again. "Trig says it's a lot harder than gunfighting, but no one's shooting back at him, so he figures that's worth something. The boys are doing real well."

The men fell silent for a moment as Devon gathered his thoughts, considering how to tell Brian about the local trouble. Katy watched him without speaking.

Richards' eyes shifted from Devon to Katy and back again. "Come out with it Devon, what's the bad news? It is late for a social visit, so I am sure there is more to your being here than making small talk about cattle."

Devon's eyes met his friend's. "There seems to be some growing resentment toward your being here."

"Really? How so?"

"I've heard some complaints and loose talk from some of the smaller ranchers and locals that 'that Englishman doesn't belong here taking up all that land.' Tonight I heard a couple of drunken men talking, saying that you stole this ranch from Sampson ... and that you should be burned out."

Richards lifted his right eyebrow and looked at Devon, "Burn me out?"

Katy grinned, "Devon took exception to what the men had to say. I don't know what happened to the second one, but the first one has a nose flatter than a skillet."

With an approving nod Richards looked at Devon, "I take it you let them know that such an undertaking would not be easy for them?"

"They got the point. Brian, I'm sure it's just some complainers looking for something to complain about, but you should be on the lookout all the same, just in case some fool actually does try to make trouble."

Katy looked over at Devon, "I think there's more to it than that. I know how all this started with us before you came, I think it's a safe bet that someone, or a few someone's, are behind this and getting folks stirred up against Brian."

Devon shook his head, "I don't know Katy, why would this be more than just complainers? What would their purpose be?"

"To take this ranch from him, Devon. They're using his being English as a justification, but there's more to it than that. Think about it once, nobody has said a bad word about Brian in over a year; most folks seem to have accepted him. Now, all of a sudden, out of nowhere, talk starts, talk that's contrary to how most people here feel. That's pretty suspicious to me and sounds like it's from outside of here."

At this point, Henry reappeared in the room with glasses of wine on a tray. As he went to each of them Richards smiled at him, "Thank you Henry. Say Henry, have you heard any rumblings on your trips to town about my being here?"

Henry thought for a moment and then shook his head, "No sir, just the usual jokes at my expense, but nothing of serious consequence."

"I'll have Bill and the men keep a look out just in case. Katy may have a valid point; someone may be instigating this for his own purposes."

Devon frowned and studied the floor. "I can't think of anyone of hand who would start that sort of trouble, oh, a few talkers will make some noise to go along with the latest rumor, but to call for burning and such, I can't think of anyone who would do that. I have to agree with Katy in that, if there is someone else involved they have to be from outside the area."

Devon studied the floor for a silent minute then raised his head, "Hold that, Farley Knolls was the second drunk in the saloon. He would be one to start something like this or at least first in line behind whoever did."

Katy looked at Devon with questioning eyes, "Farley Knolls? Do I know him?"

"Sure, you know him; he came up to our place that day saying he was Sampson's new foreman."

Katy's eyes went wide, "Him!"

"Yep, that was him, he's a two-bit hired gun. I wonder if he's been hired for this or if he's just running his mouth?"

Katy thought for a moment, "If he was hired, would he be announcing it to the whole saloon?"

"If he was drinking he might, or he could be simply siding in with whoever is involved in the talk. He might even have his own purpose in this, we did humiliate him pretty bad and he might want to get even for it."

Cupping his hand over his chin Richards stared ahead as he thought. "We have no way of knowing which, at least for now. What we need to consider is who has something to gain by getting rid of me. Just a group of grumbling jealous men talking big is no genuine threat. They have no power to take this ranch and have nothing to gain by doing so. It has been my experience that such men are unwilling to put any true effort into carrying those threats out."

"Especially if they stand a chance of getting shot for it," Devon added.

"Exactly. Why would simple complainers take that risk?"

"They wouldn't," Katy broke in, "but someone who has this ranch to gain would. Remember, Egg Taylor and Charlie Sampson had something to gain and look at the risks they took."

Devon nodded, "You're right." Then looking over at Richards he continued, "I think there is someone out there stirring this up. It doesn't make any sense for different people to suddenly get together and start bad-mouthing Brian Richards at the same time. Someone started this to stir up bad blood against you."

Richards met Devon's eyes, "I can't argue your point. It would appear that a person, or persons, has set a plan in motion to take the Juniper away from me. Now, we need to find out who and why."

"I'll talk to Trig and Hack, see what they can find out. Trig knows a lot of people who could be involved in this sort of thing, he'll know where to look."

Richards grinned, "And from the sounds of things you already drew the first blood against them."

"If they come after you Brian I can promise they'll be losing a lot more blood before this is over."

Richards stood up and walked over to a closed cabinet; opening it he removed a holstered revolver, slid the gun out and looked it over. Glancing at Devon he spoke calmly, "If they want a fight, then they can have one."

Devon's eyes widened. "That's a nice looking gun Brian, where did you get that?"

"It's called a 'Thunderer,' .41 caliber, made by Samuel Colt. Have you ever seen a double action revolver before?'

Devon shook his head and stood up, "I've heard of them, but never actually held one."

"Hold this one then," Richards handed the gun to Devon. "I bought it in Cheyenne, Wyoming, while at a cattleman's convention. I have fired it a few times. It is not battle tested yet, but I believe it will be soon."

Devon thumbed back the hammer and then carefully lowered it. Richards took the gun from him and removed the six brass cartridges, then handed it back to him. "Pull the trigger."

Devon pointed the revolver at the wall and pulled the trigger. To his amazement the hammer came back and snapped forward with the follow-through of the trigger pull. He pulled the trigger again and watched the hammer come back and snap forward. Handing the gun back to Richards he marveled at it. "That's something alright. In a gunfight saving that second in not having to thumb back the hammer could be enough to save your life."

"Exactly, it can mean all the difference."

As Richards turned the gun over and studied it, Henry walked into the room and watched him. "Expecting trouble or are we merely enjoying the feel of a fine weapon?"

"Both. Ready your weapons, my old friend. I believe we are bound for war."

To Devon's surprise Henry smiled broadly, "Very good sir, it will be good to smell the powder smoke of battle again."

Devon watched the man as he made a perfect turn off his heel and marched straight back into the adjoining room. Turning his attention to Richards, he noticed that he had taken Henry's comment as perfectly natural. He decided there was more to Henry Holden then met the eye.

Chapter 3

Besides the dealer, only two men remained at the table. The player to his right fidgeted nervously, he had lost all but a few of the dollars he had begun the game with. The dealer knew the man could ill afford to lose the money, but he didn't care. The fact that the man was anxious only made it easier to skin him clean of every dollar he owned. The stack of bills in front of him attested to more than his card playing skill.

The player directly across from the dealer was just the opposite; he was in no hurry and knew exactly what he was doing at the table. His cold black eyes rested on the man in the white shirt and slicked back hair, that he was a cheat was clear. The black eyes penetrated the dealer and made him nervous, he was afraid that the man was on to him.

He had carefully dealt him four hearts to get him to bet up his hand. Where the farmer was a timid bird for the plucking, the other was a dangerous bull. One was throwing away his family's grocery money; the other was playing money he had taken from someone else. The jet black hair and matching handlebar mustache matched the eyes and fit the man's trail hardened face.

The farmer watched, his faced clouded in fear, as the dealer threw down the last Stud card, his pained expression reflected his loss. He slumped in his chair as the dealer studied the hard eyes of the man across from him. The man never looked at his cards or the deck in the dealer's smooth hands, his eyes held those of the dealer and nothing more. Licking his lips as a nervous habit, the dealer's soft fingers and manicured nails lightly slipped a card from the bottom of the deck and laid the flush busting card face down.

The man shifted his eyes from the dealer's to the card in front of him. Lifting the corner with his left hand he looked at it and nodded slightly as if answering his own question. It was obvious he had expected the card to be anything but a heart. He flipped the deuce of spades up and returned his cold, emotionless eyes to those of the dealer. The soft hands held back, not daring to reach for the money in the center of the table. The hesitation on the dealer's part, and the nervous flickering of his eyes from side-to-side said it all.

No one in the room was paying attention to the game, so the roar of the .45 jerked everyone in the saloon straight up. All eyes turned to view the sight of the dealer's blood reddening his white shirt and pooling under him on the plank floor. The black haired man's bullet had hurtled the dealer and his chair backward leaving him sitting half in it in death.

The man calmly stood up as he counted his money out of the pot with his left hand and stuffed it in his hip pocket. Holstering the gun, he turned and walked out the door with all eyes following him. Standing outside the saloon, he pulled a sack of Bull Durham out of his pocket and rolled a smoke. Striking a match on the side of the building he lit it and studied the street.

Harper Sloan pondered the town as he smoked, it was just a little nothing place with nothing to offer him. He took the last drag on the cigarette and threw it in the dirt. He considered how the town would only be so much dust and busted down buildings in another five years. He wondered why a card sharp would even bother setting up a game here for the miserable pickings available to him, but then he wasn't any good at it anyway, probably a local grown boy.

The rest of his men were meeting him here sometime today, they had split up after the Baker City shooting. They had caught the Marshal alone on the road, but hadn't expected him to make a fight of it against eight men. He grinned as he thought back on the two bullets he had put in the lawman's back, but not before the Marshal had put one in Larry's head. Back shot, front shot, it didn't matter; the end result was that Willard Vaughn was left face down on the road and he was out of the way.

While he was waiting, he checked out the town for any potential targets. There was little to offer but grubbing miners, a few farmers, and no money. When they got back together they'd get out of this hole and head on down to Drewsey. He was anxious to get his plan into action.

He had already paid one visit to Drewsey and started talking to some of the local small ranchers and stirring up resentment against that Richards. His mouth twisted down into a frown when he considered what he had lost and that someone else now had it. He was pleased however at how easy it had been to buy a few drinks for the locals and get them fired up. He was hopeful that the seeds he had planted against Brian Richards were taking root.

While he ran the plan over in his mind, he heard the door open behind him and watched as two men carried the dead card sharp out of the saloon. They strained to hold on to the body as they went around the building and disappeared. Then the sound of several moving horses made him turn his attention back to the street. He looked up without expression at the six men mounted in front of him.

Travis Jackson looked down at him, "Well Harp, anything here for us?"

"Naw, not worth the effort. What's the word in Baker?"

Jackson grinned, "Nobody seems to know what happened to Marshal Vaughn."

Sloan's expression was sarcastic, "How tragic. Dinton take over yet?"

"Oh yeah, he just moved right in."

Sloan's eyes brightened, "Perfect, we might need him. Dinton'll do anything for fifty dollars."

"You ready to go, Harp?"

The rider to Jackson's right gave Sloan a dirty look. "I thought we were staying here for a while."

Sloan returned the look, "We're going down to Drewsey."

"Drewsey? Ain't nothing in Drewsey worth riding all that way for."

"I've got some business that needs attending to and you boys are going to help me."

"So, what's in it for us?"

"Plenty."

The rider held Sloan's cold eyes without flinching, then nodded his acceptance of the terse answer. "So, what do you want us to do?"

"Just hang around until I give you the word. I've got a pot to stir up against some fancy-pants Englishman. When we've got everything where we want it, we kill him and take what's ours. You can all have a cut of it."

The mounted men looked at each other and made comments of approval to their leader's plan. Jackson was the only man among them who knew the full story; the two gave each other a knowing look.

Stepping into the street, Sloan pulled his horse's reins loose from the hitch rail and mounted. Without another word, he turned the sorrel's nose southwest and spurred him into a lope with the six men following.

Noon of the next day found the men riding into Drewsey. They took in the cut of the town as they rode slowly alongside the rough-board buildings. Their own appearance brought little attention as the town was a gathering place for everyone. Outlaws rubbed elbows with cattlemen at the bars, and traveling men, whether lone wolves or in groups, were too common to notice. Besides, Drewsey was noted for its hard cases and men minded their own business if they wanted to keep breathing.

Sloan spotted the saloon adjoining the café and reined his horse over, he had been there before. Stepping out of the saddle, he walked through the saloon's open door, the men with him did likewise. Looking around the room, he studied the assortment of men scattered between the four walls, his gaze fell on a vacant table and he made his way to it. He sat down as five of the men with him headed for the bar; Jackson sat down across from him.

The barkeep brought a bottle and two glasses to the table in response to Sloan's gesture for them. Paying them no mind, the man dropped the glasses with a rattle and clunked the bottle next to them. Sloan tossed a pair of silver dollars on the table; the barman scooped them up as casually as he had dropped the bottle. Turning on his heels, he returned to his place behind the bar.

Several men watched the black haired man from their places in the room, among them was Mel Johns. Some of the men recognized the man for what he was; he was a stranger, but obviously an outlaw. No one spoke to him, as his business was considered to be his own and the less said to his type the better.

Mel Johns debated whether he should go talk to the man or not. He remembered him, but didn't know his name. This was the man he told Knolls he wanted to talk to, but he halted, trying to work up the nerve to approach him. He was a dangerous looking character and something in his gut warned him not to get involved with anything this man was up to, but then there was Farley Knolls to contend with. He had to get something started in regards to the Englishman or there would be Knolls to explain it to. He wasn't sure who he was most afraid of, this man or Knolls; he rose from his seat with a half empty beer glass in his hand and walked slowly toward the table.

Standing over the two seated men he looked at Sloan. "Mind if I join you?"

The outlaw looked up at Johns, "Why, you lonely?"

"I was here the day you came in last month; you were talking about the Englishman. Do you recall that?"

Pushing an empty chair out with his foot, Sloan nodded to him, "Have a seat."

Johns put the glass down and sat in the offered chair. "Some of us have been talking about what you said. You know, about how this foreigner stole Chuck's ranch. We put it together and figured you were right. We can't get Chuck out of prison, but we can get that Englishman off his place."

Sloan's eyes reflected satisfaction that the words of dissension he had planted in their heads a month ago had taken hold so nicely. "How many are in agreement with you?"

"There's six of us ranchers and a few others who don't like what happened to our neighbor, maybe a dozen all together."

"You know, if you want to take Charl ...Chuck's place back from him, you're going to have to stick together. It might even come down to a fight, maybe even gunplay, any of you up to that?"

Johns didn't care for the sound of the gunplay part, but he was committed now. He coughed nervously, "Whatever it takes. We have a few men on our side who have a reputation for using their guns, the best is Farley Knolls."

Pretending to mull over the name, Sloan nodded his head and lied, "Yeah, I've heard of him. You get Knolls on your side and you've got some fire power."

Johns leaned back in his chair, "I think we can get enough men to make this happen."

"Well, I've got six good men with me, and we intend to see that it does happen."

"Since we're going to be working together, I guess I should know your name, mine's Mel Johns."

"Harper Sloan."

Johns jerked upright in his chair, "Sloan? *The* Harper Sloan?"

"The only one I know."

Staring at the outlaw, Johns wished he had never opened his

mouth that day in the saloon. He had too much to drink and had started talking tough about running the Englishman out and it had stuck to him like glue. First, it was Knolls and now this; he was in way over his head and he wanted out, but there was no way without drawing the wrath of Knolls and ending up dead.

He wondered why this known outlaw would even care about the Englishman. He ventured the question, "Just out of curiosity, Mister Sloan, why are you interested in the Englishman, and why do you care about Chuck Sampson's place? After all, you're not from around here, and you never even knew Chuck."

Sloan shrugged his shoulders, "Let's just say I'm a concerned American citizen who sees an injustice here and wants to see it righted. I'm also concerned about the English trying to get a foothold in here and making another try at taking back this country. We've had two wars with them English already; I think it's our duty to prevent another war with them – don't you?"

The answer didn't make sense, but he wasn't about to question it further. "Sure, we have to protect ourselves and our neighbors. If this Englishman can have one of our neighbors arrested and imprisoned in order to steal his land, what chances do the rest of us have?"

With a wide smile, Sloan slapped his hand down on the table. "Exactly Mel, and that's why we're here. We have to move easy though, and not tip our hand to the enemy. You spread the word and we'll all get together and make our plans. Do you have a place we can meet?"

"I guess we can use my place to meet."

"How about tomorrow night, Mel?"

"That would be alright. Just ride south of town, and stay on the road."

"We'll be there. You're a good man, Mel."

Downing the last of his beer, Johns put the glass down and walked out of the saloon with his shoulders slightly bent. Both men watched him until he disappeared out the door. Jackson turned and looked Sloan in the face, then stifled a laugh. "You ever think of being on the stage? That was some performance, and the biggest load of bull I've ever heard heaped in one place. A concerned citizen, that was a good one."

Sloan hissed with disgust, "What an idiot! I hate stupid people who believe anything you tell them."

Jackson looked back at the door Johns had left through. "You know Harp; I'm not so sure he wants to do this. He was really nervous, someone else might be pushing him into this from another side, we'd better be paying attention."

"If someone else is thinking about moving in on this deal we'll just get rid of him when the time comes." Then, breaking into a wide grin, Sloan added, "Funny you should mention stage, we could use some spending money."

Getting up from the table, Sloan jerked his head toward the door for his men to follow. Leaving their places at the bar they wandered out behind him. As Sloan stepped out into the street, he squinted his eyes trying to adjust them to the bright sunlight and ran directly into a man walking past.

With a push and a curse he shoved the offending man away, only to have the man come back with a hard shove of his own. Tripping over his feet, Sloan flew backwards and ended up sprawled in the dirt, facing the sky. His men turned as one to brace the man who was so bold as to shove Harper Sloan.

The man hovered over the prone outlaw and coolly looked the others over with a calm and casual grin. He returned his attention to the cursing Sloan as he struggled to get up. As he made his feet, his eyes adjusted to the light and he came face to face with the man who had been standing over him.

Recognition suddenly filled Harper Sloan's face as he realized who he was looking at. "Trig Parker! Well, fancy running into you."

"Running is the word, alright. You're just as clumsy as ever."

Sloan's face darkened, but he kept the grin pasted on. He never cared much for Trig Parker, but he secretly feared his fighting abilities. They were in different classes; he was an outlaw, a robber of stages, and a sure-thing killer. Parker was a 'look-you-in-the-eye and gun you down' kind of fighter. He was also the fastest man he'd ever seen get a pistol into action. They had had a difficulty some years back in Nevada; he had come out of it clean by making Parker look the fool. That was the day he made a bad enemy of Trig Parker and he knew it. He resented the fact that he felt the need to walk and talk carefully around him now, but it was best not to push him.

Trig held the grin, "Long way from home, aren't you? The last I heard you were hiding out in the Rubies, dodging the law. What's wrong, run out of old ladies to rob down in Nevada?"

The men with Sloan knew Trig Parker by reputation, but only their leader and maybe Jackson, had ever actually met him. They watched the exchange between the two with curiosity, it was the first time they had ever seen Harper Sloan take an insult from any man.

"We've got business here."

"The only business you've ever been in is dirty business." Then giving a disapproving look to the men around him he added, "And I see you've picked up a pack of hounds to run with."

The men stared in disbelief as Sloan accepted one insult after another. Either he was scared of Parker, or they were good friends just insulting for the fun, but Parker wasn't sounding like they were friends. It was something to bear in mind. If Sloan was afraid of Parker there must be a reason.

"You might say we need to avoid anything south of us for a while. So, what are you doing here? Just passing through?"

Before Trig could answer, his brother caught up and stood next to him. Tilting his head toward Hack Trig answered, "My brother and I have a ranch north of here."

With mock surprise Sloan opened his eyes wide, "You've settled down and become respectable?"

"If need be."

Sloan's voice reflected excitement, "Then I guess you've hung up your gun and don't do that sort of thing anymore."

Trig studied Sloan for a moment. He was here for some no good reason and the tone of his question was in hopes that he would not have to contend with Trig Parker's gun in doing it. "I still pack my six-gun and have no problems in using it."

Sloan's hopeful expression disappeared as he sought to quickly change the subject. "Well, since you're a rancher now, you might have heard about this Englishman who took over Chuck Sampson's ranch."

The grin dropped off Trig's face. "Charlie Sampson's a snake's belly and nobody took over his ranch, it was bought, fair and legal."

Sloan laughed nervously; he had stepped out of one cow pie right into another one. "I take it you don't care much for this Sampson fellow."

"Sampson should have bought a bullet, or a rope, and that *Englishman* is a friend of mine. It would be a big mistake Sloan to underestimate Brian Richards, or his friends." Then resuming his customary grin Trig added, "Nevada might be a whole lot safer for you right now." Turning, Trig and Hack walked away from the outlaws.

Harper Sloan watched after them while the eyes of his men held on him. Silently he cursed to himself, shifting his eyes to Jackson he grumbled, "This just got harder."

Chapter 4

A dozen horses were tied to anything that would hold them while their riders were clustered in Mel Johns' house. Harper Sloan and his men rode quietly into the yard. Others were coming down the road, but in the darkness they couldn't make out who, or how many. They dismounted and carelessly spun their reins to the top rail of a broken down fence.

The lamps glowed behind the curtainless windows highlighting the heads and motions of the men in the room behind the glass. Sloan gave the place a quick look around; it was rundown. Even in the dark he could make out the clutter of cast off wagon pieces, broken fences, and the sagging porch roof of the house. He might be an outlaw, but he was a clean man and had no respect for those who just threw everything around. He was willing to overlook it however for the opportunity to twist Mel Johns around his finger and use him to get the Englishman off the ranch.

Ducking under the sagging roof rafters of the porch, he opened the door and stepped into the brightly lit room. The attention of the men turned to focus on him. All conversation ceased as Harper Sloan was suddenly of more interest than the price of cattle. He noticed that the house was little better than the yard had been.

Breaking into a false smile, he reached his hand out to Johns. "Mel, good to see you, and I see your friends are here too. I've got to thank you for inviting us."

Travis Jackson tossed Sloan a sidelong glance and rolled his eyes back.

Johns accepted Sloan's outstretched hand, feeling a twinge of pride that someone as famous as Harper Sloan was treating him like a friend in front of the others. "The men have been looking forward to meeting you. Come over here and I'll introduce you to Farley Knolls."

Leading the outlaw up to Knolls, Johns' expression was tense in regards to the two gunmen meeting. "Farley, this is Harper Sloan, the man I was telling you about."

Farley had been drinking enough to be unsteady on his feet and to slow his already witless mind. He stared at the man in front of him, while trying to stand straight and look intimidating. He was the cock-of-the-walk around here and wasn't about to play second fiddle to Sloan. "Harper Sloan, I've heard of you."

Mentally Sloan shook his head in disgust, he didn't need a drunk with a gun blowing the plan he had been building piece-by-piece for months. He glared at Knolls, "You always drunk?"

Knolls stared back hard at the outlaw, who stood several inches taller then he did, trying to match his glare. He wasn't sure if that was a question or an insult. "I can handle my liquor, you some kind of Sunday School teacher or something?" He laughed at his imagined cleverness.

Sloan's eyes never shifted off those of Knolls, "I don't need a drunk with a big mouth getting in the way."

Johns shifted his feet uneasily; he was starting to think that Sloan and Knolls were going to shoot it out right in his house. He knew how obnoxious Farley Knolls could be and didn't blame Sloan, but he didn't need them going at each other here and now. Then again, maybe Sloan would kill Knolls and rid him of the major source of his problems; he wondered whether he should just let him, but he thought better of it. Quickly stepping in between the two men, Johns invited Sloan to turn around and meet some of the other men in the room. "I'm sorry about Farley, he can be like that sometimes, but I'm sure he will be valuable to you."

With a nod Sloan grinned at Johns, "I'm sure he'll do fine for us."

Looking back over his shoulder, Sloan locked eyes with the sneering Knolls. He decided that Knolls was a problem to be eliminated at the first opportunity. He'd find a way to kill him and twist it to their purpose. Maybe this so-called gunman might be useful after all, useful dead. In the meantime Mel Johns and his friends didn't need to suspect that he had a problem with their hero, Mister Knolls.

One by one, Johns went to each man in the house giving them a chance to shake the hand of Harper Sloan. Most were excited that this famous man had come to help them fight the foreigner who had stolen Chuck Sampson's ranch. No one stopped to question why he was there and Sloan was pleased with their ignorance.

Outwardly he gave the appearance of being happy to meet them; inwardly he despised them for being weak minded fools. Fool enough to completely accept a bill of goods sold to them by a total stranger and so weak that they had to constantly be talking their courage up about running Richards out. He knew they would be huddled behind him and his men like a bunch of children hiding behind their mother. He intended to change that though.

The latest man he was introduced to was talking to him, but he didn't hear him as his own thoughts covered the man's babbling. The thought briefly crossed his mind that these people might be putting on an act of their own to get him to do their dirty work for them. He considered Jackson's remark about someone using Johns to work out his own deal. Maybe that's where Farley Knolls came into the picture. In the end it wouldn't matter anyway, when he was done with them he'd crush all of them under his boot like so many scorpions.

His mind came back to the conversation as the next man he was led up to came into focus. The man's swollen and bruised face caught his full attention. He studied the man for a moment, that he had received a beating from someone was obvious. "You get run over by a train or something?"

Johns answered for the man, "This is Chic Took, he has a place south of here. He ran into Devon McCloud – a friend of Brian Richards."

Glancing over at Johns Sloan frowned, "Who's Devon McCloud?" The condition of Took's face made a statement all its own about this McCloud.

"He's the foreman of the Bitter Grass; they had a grudge against Chuck. There was a big shootout up at their place with some of Chuck's hands. That's when Richards came in with the Marshal and arrested Chuck and took over his place. Chic here was speaking his mind about Richards and McCloud didn't like it."

"This McCloud, is he a tough character or does he just think he is?"

Johns looked perplexed, "He's a tough one alright. Hear tell he's some kind of a gunfighter and he's a real pal with Richards and that Parker outfit."

Sloan involuntarily jerked upright, "Trig Parker?"

"Yeah, their old man was a cattle thief and a no-account drunk. I can't say his boys are any better. McCloud helped set them up in the cattle business with some of Chuck's cattle. Their place borders his."

Running this new information through his mind, Sloan held the frown. He knew Parker was going to be a problem; and now there was this McCloud who sounded about as bad. He might have to get rough right off before they could get set, but he wanted to try something first. He wanted to see if these friends of Johns' could put enough pressure on Richards to scare him out. He had always heard that the English were a lot of tea drinking sissies. He wanted to see just how much Richards could take before tucking his tail and running off.

"Mel, if these Parkers are known cattle thieves and McCloud is a friend of theirs, and even helped them get set up with another man's cattle, is there any chance McCloud is a cattle thief ,too?"

Johns rubbed his chin, "That could be. They're a secretive lot up there on the mountain. Some think Chuck was on to them rustling his cattle and that's what the fight was all about. It is possible that McCloud, those Parkers, and that Englishman are all mixed together in the same pot. We already know they have Chuck's Wire Creek cattle all over their spreads, it could well be that they're running rustled cattle."

Sloan could feel his chest swell as he patted himself on the back. The seed he just planted was brilliant, now suspicion was cast on the whole lot of Richards' friends. These men would talk it up, stretch it, make up lies, and then hopefully act on it. If they did it right, they could destroy Richards and McCloud in one swipe and then he'd just step in and take over.

"Sounds about right to me, Mel. Talk it over with your friends and see if they don't all agree and can find some proof of this matter."

Sloan glowed with triumph and was about to expand on the rustling idea when he was interrupted by Farley Knolls. The drunken slur to the man's voice set his nerves on edge. "I always knew there was something about that McCloud I didn't like. It's all coming clear now, they've been rustling cattle right under our noses and we never suspected. Now that we know for a fact that's what they're doing, we'll make a quick end to them."

John's let out an exasperated sigh, "We don't know that for a *fact,* Farley."

Lifting his chin in the direction of Chic Took, Farley went on. "That's why McCloud smashed up Chic's face like that. I was with him, we were talking about Richards taking over Chuck's place when all of sudden McCloud comes busting into the place and just let ol' Chic have it without so much as a word of warning."

Stepping into the conversation, Took spoke slowly through his swollen lips, "That's right; we were just talking and the next thing I knew McCloud up and hits me. I owe him for this and I intend to collect, with interest."

Straining to look concerned and not break into a laugh, Sloan studied the three men. "I can't see why you men allow these people to just run roughshod all over you like this. Cattle thefts, land thefts, and then trying to kill a man just because he was brave enough to speak out about it. If I were you, I'd be riding out to that Englishman's house and letting him know it won't be stood for any longer."

All the men in the house were now gathered around Sloan listening to his speech. He turned and looked at the men who were standing stone silent. He knew exactly what was going on in their minds; they had talked it up, but didn't have the nerve to actually do something about it. He had put them in a position to either put up or shut up. He waited in equal silence for some kind of reply.

An older man in the group was the first to speak out. "I know we all came here to talk about this matter and see how each of us felt. Some liked Chuck, some of us didn't. We all have our concerns about what the Englishman is all about and that's why I'm here. I'm interested in how my neighbors feel about all this."

Sloan studied the man for a long minute, he was gray haired with a tough, weathered face. He had been around and it was plain that this old man wasn't going to be ramrodded into anything.

"Well then, what do you think about it all?"

Israel Dodd held the outlaw's eyes, his own sharp clear eyes never flinched, he didn't like Harper Sloan one bit. "I think two things about it. First, I ain't running off half-cocked on anything, and second, where do you fit into all this? Why should we listen to you?"

Dodd had been in the country longer than any of them and was respected by the majority of the men in the room; he had a level head and knew how to use it. When others were jumping into something, Israel Dodd was thinking it out first before he decided. He struck a note of sense to those few men in the room who shared his way of thinking.

Another rancher spoke out, "You're not from here Sloan, why

should you care about any of this? I say you've got your own game going on here for your own benefit."

"I'm with Pat." All eyes turned back to Dodd. "I've talked to Devon McCloud a time or two and I'm a good judge of men. McCloud is no cattle thief. When it comes right down to it *Mister* Sloan, ain't you a fine one to be callin' the kettle black? You're a known outlaw and thief yourself and here you are accusing other men you don't even know of being thieves. Now ain't that a fine affair?"

Johns gave Dodd a worried look and tried to show his support for Knolls and Sloan. "Can't you see it Israel? It all adds up."

"To what? To this darn outlaw pretending to care about the goings on here? You've never been too bright anyway Mel, *try* and use your own pea brain and think about it. This man comes in here, out of nowhere, talking about something he shouldn't even know anything about and you just swallow it all up. If these people were rustling cattle don't you think we'd have figured that out ourselves by now? Besides, Sam Raven's Brian Richards' manager; I suppose you think he's a cattle thief too? Ain't he supposed to be a friend of yours, Mel?"

John's felt his stomach knot up. Sam *was* a friend of his and here he was siding in with this outfit against him. He felt trapped, with no safe way to turn. He knew Israel was right, but he lacked the courage to say so.

Dodd gave him a chance to answer; but when Johns remained silent he finished his statement. "Do you really think we need this no-account outlaw coming in here and telling us what to do?" Dodd's temper was beginning to heat up.

Sloan ignored the old man, refusing to acknowledge his accusations. Straightening his back he looked the group over and spoke. "Men, the bottom line here is whether or not you believe your livelihoods are at risk from this Englishman and his gunfighter friends. Do you want them out of your country and out of your lives or do you want them here where everyday you run the risk of ending up like Chuck Sampson?"

"Hogwash!" Dodd spit back at him. "You people are acting like Sampson was some kind of a saint or something. If you men were to be honest with yourselves, you all can recall bad mouthing Charlie Sampson at one time or another. He was never a neighbor to any of us and if anyone was a cattle thief, it was *him*."

Harper Sloan's eyes filled with fire. Glaring at Dodd he hissed through clenched teeth, "I think you've worn out your welcome here, old man."

Holding eyes with the outlaw Dodd knew he had touched a nerve, a very raw nerve. It confirmed his suspicions that there was more to Harper Sloan's involvement then he let on. "I'm leavin', not because you said to, but because I won't have any part in this business. I'm not riding against my neighbors based on the word of an outlaw." Then turning his attention back to the men surrounding him his voice took on a warning tone. "You suit yourselves, but mark my words; you will all pay dearly if you follow this man."

As he turned to walk out, Pat Lyons broke out of the pack and followed him. A murmur filled the room as the two men walked angrily out of the house.

Mel Johns made a desperate attempt to call after them, but it was a futile effort, the two men had heard enough and had no intentions of stopping or looking back. The slamming door silenced the room.

"Aw, let 'em go," Farley Knolls waved after them. "Who needs 'em? We've got all the men we need right here without those two mama's boys."

Voices once again began to fill the house, but now they were splitting into factions. Feeling the dissent spreading through the room, Sloan quickly put his hands in the air and called out, "Men, let's get back to business here. We need to be organized and together on this."

Farley shouted out above the talk, "Shut up!"

The men stopped as one and turned their attention to Knolls. He was wavering slightly side-to-side and his eyes had the dull look of a man who had been drinking too much. "Which of you in this room has the guts to stand up to this Englishman and his pals? If your guts have run out and you're yellow, then get out of here."

He paused and glared at the group. No one moved; even if they wanted to they were frozen in place at the threat of being branded cowards. Several of the men who were the most adamant about running Richards out shouted in approval of Sloan and his plan.

Knolls put his hands on his hips and grinned, "That's more like it." Then casting a smug glance toward Sloan he concluded, "There's your men."

Chapter 5

Bill Anthony and Sam Raven rode to either side of their boss as they surveyed the changing scene of the old Wire Creek place. It was now the eastern half of the Juniper Cattle Company, or Juniper East as it was commonly known by the men who worked it.

Brian Richards had given both of his managers every detail of the talk he had had with the McClouds. It was not lost on them that Richards, who had customarily gone unarmed, was now never seen without the Colt belted around his waist. That fact alone convinced the men that their boss was taking the threats seriously and therefore they did as well. Wearing a gun was a part of their everyday dress, but now they knew that it was necessary to be ready to use them.

The horses moved slowly through the sage as the men took in the details of the grass sprouting up between the bushes. Coming up to one of the new ditches, they could see that the summer was having its effect and drying it down to a couple of inches of slow moving water. Sitting silently on their horses each man cast a glance toward Richards who looked across the land with something that seemed like affection.

In a low voice Bill broke the silence, "Place is shaping up real nice, Mister Richards."

With a nod he turned his head toward Bill. "Yes it is. You have done a fine job of bringing this range back up from nothing."

Sam stepped off his horse and picked at a cluster of grass, pulling it up he studied the roots. "Looks healthy, it's taking hold real good. It's up to you Mister Richards, but I'd leave it alone for the winter and then by spring start moving some cattle on it."

Richard's turned toward Bill, "I was thinking this fall, but it is your management Bill, what do you think?"

"Sam's one of the best range managers I've ever met, I have to agree with him Mister Richards. Give this grass a chance to root down hard over the winter and by spring we should have one first rate range."

"Then that is what we will do. I will trust the two of you to oversee the progress."

As one, the three men spotted the high dust cloud moving toward the house from the northeast. Sam stood up from his crouched position and narrowed his eyes trying to make out the source. "Takes a lot of riders moving fast to raise a cloud like that and I'd bet my summer wages they're not coming to invite us to a birthday party."

The look on Richard's face turned hard as his brow furrowed deeply. "No, I doubt it as well, and neither are they invited to one here."

Kicking his horse into a gallop, he raced through the sage keeping the bay's nose pointed directly at the house a half mile away. Bill waited for Sam as he grabbed his saddlehorn and threw himself up and into the saddle. In seconds they were directly on the heels of Richards' horse.

Reaching the ranch yard, Richards slid his horse to a stop between the house and the oncoming riders. His two men pulled up to either side of him and watched the riders approach. They could now make out eight mounted men, but not their faces. Another few seconds and they were in the yard.

Pulling their horses down to a walk, the riders kept moving forward as the lathered horses dug deep for air. Sam knew the men, a few he had considered to be friends. They were all strangers to Bill and Richards.

Leaning forward in the saddle, Richards shouted out to the riders. "You men are on my property, if your intentions are peaceful then you are welcome, if not your welcome stops right there."

The men kept moving forward until the noses of their horses were only a few feet from the three mounted riders blocking their progress toward the house. Coming to a halt, the two lines faced each other in silence.

Sam rested his left elbow on the saddlehorn and leaned over his horse's neck. "You boys have business here?"

Mel Johns shifted nervously as he tried to think of something to say. Sam was his friend and now he was faced up against him; he sorely regretted being there. He wished he had the nerve to stand up to Knolls and Sloan, if he did he'd be lined up with Sam Raven instead of with the side he knew was wrong. He had talked himself into a bad situation and didn't have the guts to ride out. Now, he was facing three armed and dangerous men, one of whom was a friend and he was with a rag-tag bunch of jealous little men.

Sam locked his eyes on Johns who was trying desperately not to meet his friend's gaze. "I never expected you to be riding with this rabble, Mel."

Farley Knolls forced his horse forward. "We come to run this Englishman out of the country."

Sam turned a hard glare on Knolls. "You tried that once already, you recall the Chaney place? You ever get your tail pulled back out?"

"What's that supposed to mean?"

"You had your tail sucked up so hard between your legs running out of there I figured it'd take a doctor to get it back out for you"

Knolls' face flushed red, he knew what Sam Raven said was true, but he had no intentions of letting anyone else know it. "I ought'a kill you for that Raven."

"You *ought* to, but you won't and you and I both know why – don't we?"

Bill Anthony sidestepped his horse several feet to the right of Richards.

Knolls shouted at him, "What you think you're doing, trying to surround us?"

Bill never answered; he just casually flipped the loop off the hammer of his six-gun and looked at him.

Swallowing hard, Knolls looked from one expressionless face to the next and realized that they had not intimidated the Englishman or the other man at all. He already knew all about Sam Raven and had taken a big risk in challenging him. He also knew that they would all end up dead if they continued to push this any further.

"Why do you feel I need to be run out of the country?"

Knolls' attention came back to Brian Richards. He groped for words but came up empty until another loud voice saved him from further humiliation.

"Because you stole Chuck Sampson's ranch, that's why."

Richards turned his head slightly to find the speaker in the group. His searching eyes stopped on the ruddy face of a big man mounted on a little sorrel mare that was straining under her load. "I *bought* this property, you overstuffed toad. Your friend Sampson was the one trying to steal land, Abby Chaney's, and kill her to do it. He was also paying Cab Parker to steal her cattle. If there is a thief in this country it appears to be your friend Mister Sampson, and that's why he went to prison."

"You're a liar, you damned Englishman. We know that you and that McCloud, and those Parkers with him, have been rustlin' cattle."

Brian Richards' eyes narrowed as he locked a hard glare on the big man. "You have two choices sir; you can step off that horse and take a beating or draw your gun and have me shoot you. You decide which; I am perfectly comfortable with either."

The man laughed out loud. "No man has ever whupped me in a fight. Step down off that horse your own self, you sissy Englishman, and take your own beating."

Quickly dismounting, Richards unbuckled his gunbelt and handed it up to Sam. The big man struggled off his horse and then lumbered toward Richards with a smug grin. Looking like a bear, the man clenched his hands into fists the size of a draft horse's hooves and let fly with a wide roundhouse right.

The punch missed as Richards easily sidestepped it. The man growled his displeasure and swung again with the same results. With his temper growing, he charged in swinging wide punches that succeeded only in moving the air in front of Richards as he lightly stepped back. Sweat was beginning to run down the man's broad jowls while his eyes reflected confusion. He had never swung and not connected a blow like this before; he wasn't sure what to do next. Brian Richards made the decision for him.

Stepping into the man with his left fist up, Richards proceeded to land one left jab after another into the man's bewildered face. With trip-hammer timing, the blows smacked loud in the hot still air. Blood trickled down the man's face as his eyes began to swell shut. The jabs were solidly landed taking their toll on the big man; when his knees began to shake Richards stepped in and landed a solid right to the head followed by a left to the ear. The man went down like a pole-axed steer.

The man's companions stared on with their mouths hanging open.

Richards stepped back and looked the mounted riders over. "Anyone else wish to call me a liar or a thief?"

No one moved or answered.

"I thought as much. I have heard the threats that you are making, how you are going to burn me out. I give no quarter to threats or the cowards who make them. You men have worn out your welcome, it is time for you to leave or be shot as trespassers, but think about this on your way home: this will be the last time I will fight with my fists, from now on anyone of you seen on my property will be shot on sight."

Knolls stammered as he tried to form his words. "We just want to look at your cattle and see if there are any that don't belong there."

"They all belong here you dim-witted fool!" Sam shot back at him.

Knolls tried to look tough, but the fear in his eyes proved otherwise. "I mean any of Chuck's cattle."

Sam shook his head in exasperation. "Of course there's cattle from Sampson's herd; they came with the purchase of the ranch and we have legal papers to prove it."

"Well maybe, but ...."

"But nothing!" Richards tone was angry and impatient. "You are obviously an idiot and I am not in the habit of bantering words with an idiot." Reaching up to Sam, Richards took back his gunbelt, buckled it on and slid the revolver out of the holster. "I told you once to leave and now I have finished talking."

Knolls' eyes opened wide as he stared down at the gun that was now pointed at him. Yanking on the reins, he spun his horse around and left the yard in a gallop with each of the other men following in silence.

The big man was beginning to move, groaning in pain as he did. Richards toed him in the ribs. "You had better get on your horse and follow your friends."

Shakily the man rose to his knees and tried to focus his eyes through the swelling flesh around them. He managed to find his horse and clumsily crawl into the saddle. Sitting in the saddle, the man tried to find his direction.

Taking the horse by the bridle, Richards turned him toward the disappearing riders. "Go that way; your horse will catch up to them."

Straining to see Richards, the battered man whispered through his split lips. "Mister, no man has ever whupped me and I ain't never took no beating like this one." Reaching his hand down to

Richards he added, "You're alright Richards, you're a man for the country."

Accepting the man's hand Richards smiled, "Come back again – as a friend and not an enemy."

Forcing a smile the man chuckled, "I just might do that, and you've got a friend in Kenny Weaver."

Chapter 6

The four heifers wearing Trig and Hack Parker's Six Gun brand grazed lazily among the dozen or so Bitter Grass cattle. Devon had found the break in the fence and the tracks indicating that some of Parkers animals had gone through it. It took a good two hours to find them, but here they were. Making his way above the group, Devon cut the 6G cattle out of his and started them for their home pasture.

As he followed them he chuckled to himself about the brand. Trig had made a lot of changes in the past year, from gunfighter to responsible cattleman, but the brand was not only part of Trig's sense of humor, it also served as a warning to anyone who thought about rustling those cattle. Trig Parker might have stopped hiring out his gun, but he had no problems with using it when he needed to. No man in his right mind would want to be in possession of a 6G cow.

The freshly peeled pine poles of the gate that separated the two ranches was more than a gate, it was a symbol of an alliance and friendship that was forged during the bitter days of the war with Sampson and Taylor. The Parkers were solid friends, but deadly foes. These were men you wanted on your side.

Opening the gate, he pushed the willing heifers through the opening and onto their own graze. Reining his horse around, he shoved the gate closed and dropped the wire loop over the top post to hold it shut. Turning the black mare back around, he found himself facing two hard- eyed men. He sat casually in the saddle and gave them the same look back.

The man on the right pointed at the heifers, "Stealing those cattle?"

"Might be, what's it to you?"

"Plenty, since I own 'em."

"Hear tell Trig Parker owns them cattle and he's one sawed-off, milk toast excuse for a man."

The man doing the talking looked over to the younger man on his right. "Hack, you ever hear that about Trig Parker?"

The younger man nodded, "Yep, I did."

"From where?"

Pointing at Devon he spoke slowly, "From him."

The man turned his attention back to Devon. "Devon, you been bad-mouthing me again?"

Holding out his hands in front of him Devon vigorously shook his head, "Not me, I'd be too scared to talk bad about Trig Parker."

Trig Parker burst out laughing, "Like the devil you would! If I recall, we met like this about a year go, and if memory serves me right, you were threatening to blow me out of the saddle."

Devon pretended to ponder the statement, "No, don't recall such an event; you must have me mixed up with someone who wasn't your friend."

Trig laughed again, "You coming up to the cabin and have some coffee?"

Rolling his eyes back Devon groaned, "You trying to poison me again?"

"Well excuse me, I guess you've just gotten spoiled having a woman make your coffee for you these days."

A grin cut Devon's face, "Yeah, guess I'm spoiled."

"You know McCloud, if Katy wasn't my cousin . . ."

"Yeah, I know, you would have tried to take her away from me and I would have had to shoot you dead and we wouldn't be sitting here having this pleasant conversation right now. So, are you going to poison me with your coffee or just run your mouth all day?"

"Well, since we are kin and all ..." Turning his horse around, Trig stopped and looked back over his shoulder at Devon. "Milk toast?"

Devon shrugged his shoulders, "Sounded good."

The three men rode in silence through the pines, listening as a habit to the sounds around them. The country was becoming more settled and there were fewer dangers to take a man's life, but old habits died hard for men who had survived by using all their senses. Reaching the cabin, they dismounted and tied the horses off to the hitch rail.

Studying the cabin, Devon thought back on the day it was built. He and Katy were joined by Brian and several of his men. They had the Parker's new home up in a day and smoke coming out of the chimney by dark. It had been a good year for all of them, but now a new threat seemed to be looming on the horizon and it was their turn to come to the aid of Brian Richards.

Following Trig and Hack into the cabin, Devon left the door open to let in some air as the day was sizing up to be a hot one. He sat down at the table and watched Hack for a moment as he threw a chunk of wood in the stove and dipped the coffee pot into the wooden bucket filled with water. Coffee was poured out of the Arbuckles sack into the pot which was then left on the stovetop to boil.

Hack turned around to find Devon staring absently out the open door. "What's up, Devon? You look like a man worrying a problem."

As Devon turned his head back to look up at Hack, Trig stepped up next to his brother. "Something going on?"

"I think so. Either of you hear any bad talk lately about Brian?"

Trig scratched his chin as he mulled over the question. "Not that I can think of off hand."

"Yeah, we did Trig. When we were in town the other day, remember, that fella you were talkin' to? He said something about Brian."

Trig met his brother's eyes, "I forgot about that. I just figured it was more of Harper's blow-hard talk."

Devon's full attention was now on Trig. "Who's Harper and what kind of talk?"

"Harper Sloan. I ran into him in town the other day; he asked if I knew anything about that Englishman who *stole* Charlie Sampson's ranch."

"I've heard that name, friend of yours?"

Trig laughed, "Hardly. He's a two-bit stage robber and back-shooter. Actually I hate his guts – always have. We had a run-in some time back."

Devon leaned back in his chair, lifting the front legs off the floor. "Why would Harper Sloan be asking about Brian and why would he care about Sampson? Especially to the point of accusing Brian of stealing the property?"

"I don't know, but I can tell you one thing though, Harper Sloan doesn't get into anything unless he can get some money out of it."

Dropping the chair legs back down on the floor Devon stood up. "Then, I guess we need to be finding out why he's here."

"One thing to keep in mind Devon, Sloan might be two-bit and a backshooter, but he can be a mighty dangerous man and he never rides alone. He had some men with him when we saw him and if he's behind any trouble, you can bet he'll be getting more."

"Well, it's not my way to go easy, and I want to know before anything happens to Brian. I want to find out why he's here stirring up trouble."

Trig's eyes danced with amusement, "I never said go easy. I'd just as soon shoot Harper Sloan between the eyes as to look at him. I just meant don't take him lightly."

"Oh, I don't intend to take him lightly, but I will be talking to him."

"I told him I was behind Brian and he didn't seem to like that too much. Maybe now's as good a time as any to go rattle his cage some and find out why that upset him."

"I think you're both missing something."

Devon and Trig turned their attention to Hack. Their expressions asked the question.

"Why should a longtime outlaw like Harper Sloan even know a big cattleman like Charlie Sampson? And know him good enough to know all about Brian getting his ranch, and then to come all the way up here from Nevada to do something about it? Why?"

The two men looked at each other. "Little brother's got a point there."

Devon nodded, "He's right. Why would Sloan know all about Sampson's business?"

"That is interesting isn't it? Let's go ask him."

The scowl on Harper Sloan's face never changed as he silently shifted his eyes from Mel Johns to Farley Knolls. Travis Jackson sat to his left at the saloon table; he waited in his typical relaxed state as Sloan did his best to intimidate the two men. From the nervous look each man was trying to hide he figured Harper was succeeding.

The outlaw's shifting glare finally settled on Knolls. "Tell me again how an Englishman and two cowhands managed to run the whole bunch of you off?"

"They got the drop on us."

Jackson smiled as Sloan tossed a sidelong glance at him. "They got the drop on you? That always seems to be your excuse."

"Richards beat up Kenny Weaver."

Sloan's head slowly turned toward Johns' He shrugged his shoulders, "And that means what? How many of you were there again?"

"Eight."

"Eight? Seven of you watched this Englishman beat the ears off one of your men and you just sat there?"

Johns swallowed and searched desperately for an answer. How could he admit to Sloan that they were scared to death and that he didn't even want to be there? None of them had expected to encounter three armed men ready to shoot the lot of them and Kenny was the only man willing to stand up and fight. His silence was answer enough for Sloan.

"I thought as much." He returned his glare to Knolls. "I thought you were the gunman here?"

"I told you, they got the drop on us. Only a fool draws against three cocked forty-fives."

Sloan knew the man was lying. He nodded his head slightly as he held a lock on Knoll's eyes. He knew Farley Knolls was a coward and a liar. He confirmed his earlier conclusion that he would kill Knolls before this was over.

"I guess you men were just not up to the job. My men are, next time *we'll* go out there and clean this business up."

Mel Johns was as slow as Israel Dodd had accused him of, but this was all beginning to sink in. Harper Sloan did have his own plan, just like Israel had said. He hesitated as he spoke, indicating his nervousness. "I thought you had come to help us!"

A sudden burst of fury crossed Sloan's face, but he caught himself before he said the wrong thing. "I am Mel, I only meant that my men are used to this, you're not. I have only myself to blame for sending you out there. We should have taken care of this ourselves and not put you in danger."

The suspicion that had been growing in his mind was tempered by Sloan's kind words. Maybe he did honestly care about Chuck and only wanted to make things right, but he still wondered why. He decided this was a good opportunity to try and back out of the whole thing and give it to Sloan and his men. "Maybe you're right Mister Sloan; we aren't fighters, just ranchers. I'm sure you could do a much better job of this than us. We could still support you though."

Putting on his best theatrical expression of appreciation Sloan smiled, "That would be a big help Mel. Knowing you're behind us would mean a lot."

Travis Jackson shifted in his chair and muffled a forced cough with his hand to keep from bursting into laughter. The warning in Sloan's sudden glance told him to make sure he didn't.

With his hand still over his mouth, Jackson was the first one to notice Farley Knoll's eyes widen in fear and the color drain from his face as he focused his attention on something across the room. He looked to his right to see three men walking toward them. He recognized Trig Parker and his brother from the encounter Sloan had with him the day they got here, but he didn't know the third man.

Catching the change on everyone's face, Sloan turned around to see Trig Parker closing in on them. From the no nonsense look of the man next to him he figured it had to be Devon McCloud. He cursed under his breath.

They came around the table, with the Parkers each taking a position to the right and left of Harper Sloan while Devon stood behind Knolls looking directly at him. It was a full minute before Sloan chuckled and looked to his right at Trig. "Hi Trig, miss me? Had to come and visit?"

"No, we aren't here to visit and you know that if I had the chance I would never miss you."

Sloan studied Trig's face and knew what he meant.

Devon's voice broke in between them. "We want to know why you're making trouble for Brian Richards."

Pushing back in his chair, Sloan turned from Trig and looked up at the man standing across the table from him. "I don't think I know you."

"Devon McCloud – answer the question."

"Why do you care?"

Devon stared hard at the outlaw. "We're not here to play games with you, Sloan. I'll tell you this only one time. Saddle up and head back to where you came from."

"And if I don't?"

"There won't be a second warning."

A chuckle came with Sloan's growing grin. "That sounds every bit like a threat. You sure you can back it up?"

"You're burning daylight Sloan; you'd better get a move on and take this trash with you."

Farley Knolls began to get up from his seat when Devon put a solid hand on his shoulder and slammed him back down in his chair. "Best stay put Farley or you might get what your drinking pal got."

Knolls felt his bones crack as he met the chair's seat under Devon's driving hand. The wind blew out of his lungs as he winced from the pain.

The next sound they heard was the deadly metallic click of Hack's .45 as he held it behind Travis Jackson's ear. "Let it fall," Hack whispered behind him.

Jackson's surprised expression was followed by the heavy thud of his gun hitting the board floor. "That's a good boy."

Hack looked to his left at Devon, "We weren't payin' attention here, but we're all ready to listen to you now." Poking the .45's bore harder into Jackson's ear he added, "Aren't we?"

Devon looked at Jackson and then back to Sloan. "You two just got on my bad side. Time for you to leave."

"When we've finished our business we'll leave."

"What is your business?"

"To get Chuck Sampson's ranch back from that Englishman."

"Is that a fact? How do you plan to pull that off?"

"By any means necessary."

Devon put his fists down on the table and leaned over it looking into Harper Sloan's face. "It'll be a heckuva fight."

Sloan stood up and leaned into Devon until their faces were only inches apart. "Whatever it takes, right down to the last man standing."

"I'll make you one promise Sloan – it won't be you."

Chapter 7

Mel Johns stared in his shaving mirror and wondered about the man who was looking back at him. How had he come to be in this position? At what point in his life had he become gutless, unable to stand up for himself? Cowering in fear of a piece of human trash like Farley Knolls.

Here he was the unwilling leader of a group of small ranchers and townsmen who, for their own personal reasons, harbored a grudge against Brian Richards. A grudge brought on more from liquor and jealousy than any actual thing Richards had done. They were not fighters or gunmen; they didn't even have the nerve to finish their confrontation with Richards. He furrowed his brow, why were they doing this at all?

He turned away from the mirror, not sure he liked what he saw. For the first time in his life, he was face-to-face with men who were warriors. He never thought of himself as a coward until now, when he faced men who were not. These were men who handled a gun like it was a normal everyday action. All he and the others had ever done was talk; none of them had actually handled guns except for hunting. Shooting at another man, or worse yet being shot at, was a world away from shooting a deer.

He knew nothing of Brian Richards really, only that he was a foreigner and an outsider, but he knew the reputations of Devon McCloud and Trig Parker and they scared him. His witnessing of the ice cool Devon McCloud going nose-to-nose with Harper Sloan and never flinching was unnerving. What had they gotten themselves into? He wanted no part of McCloud or the Parkers.

Then there was Sloan himself and the words of Israel Dodd once again echoed in his ears. Why *did* he care about helping them? There was more to it than what the outlaw had been telling them, and it was taking hold in his mind and repeating itself over and over. He and the others were puppets for Sloan; he could see that now. Like that Jackson pal of Sloan's, always silent, watching, laughing behind his eyes. It had started out bad and was quickly getting worse. It was time to talk to the others and get them out of this before they all got killed.

The camp used by Sloan and his men was tucked against a high wall of sand and stone formed over the years by the rushing spring floods, the junipers growing on the bank above it offered concealment. Harper Sloan sat in front of the coffee fire and scowled into it. He was angry over the meeting with McCloud and Parker. Not only was there one Parker to contend with, now there were two of them. That brother of Trig's was obviously cut out of the same cloth, his poking that .45 in Jackson's ear was proof of that.

Travis Jackson sat across from the fire casually peeling the bark off a juniper twig piece-by-piece and tossing it into the fire. Every few seconds he lifted his eyes to look at Sloan, they had sat like this for over an hour. He had seen Sloan go into dark moods, but this one was the worst he'd ever seen him in and he had ridden with Harper for almost twenty years. He figured that it must be a Sloan trait, his brother was just like him.

"We going to sit here all day; you keeping that fire going with your eyes and me peeling sticks?"

Sloan raised his eyes without moving, "I'm thinking."

"About what?"

"About how to get McCloud and Parker out of the picture."

Jackson shrugged, "Shoot 'em."

"No, it's got to look honest. I don't need to hang a big sign around my neck telling the world that we gunned down a couple of well known ranchers. No, it's got to be in a way no one will connect to us."

Tossing the last of a juniper stick into the fire Jackson grinned, "Let's get Norm to arrest them for stealing Charlie's cattle. They did admit to having Wire Creek branded cattle on their property didn't they?"

Nodding his head Sloan stared back into the fire. "You just might have something there. Give Norm fifty bucks and he'd put a rope around his own mother's neck."

"Send a wire Harp, get him down here."

"Yeah, and he could appoint us his *special deputies* to help him out."

"You got it, and we come out looking like good men helping to rid the country of a bunch of cattle rustlers."

Sloan stood up from the fire, the scowl replaced by a triumphant grin. "We can get Johns and his bunch of old ladies to keep Richards busy while we get rid of his allies. By the time he figures it out, McCloud and Parker will be all the way to Baker City — in jail."

Jackson stood up and grinned back, "What are we waiting for, let's go send a telegram."

Sloan's camp was a half hour ride from Drewsey; it had been barely that when the two outlaws rode past the saloon. Both men recognized the collection of horses tied off to the rails with Mel Johns' chestnut right in the middle of them.

Jackson glanced to his left and then back to Sloan, "Looks like the boys are having a meeting."

"And without inviting us. I don't like the look of this; we'd better make sure they understand the rules here."

Reining their horses to the side of the street, the two men dismounted and made their way through the saloon door. Johns was at the far back table with several other men surrounding him, some seated, some standing. They all turned as one when Sloan stepped into the circle. Johns felt his stomach shrivel and his mouth go bone dry.

The men fell back a step as they withered under the outlaw's glare. After slowly looking at each man his glare came to rest on Mel Johns seated to his left at the table. "You boy's having a meeting?"

The group remained silent while Sloan's glare continued to penetrate Johns' fear-filled eyes. "No answer? I take it then that I probably won't like what you boys have to say."

Boots shuffled on the floor as each man fought for an answer. They had talked big that night at Johns' house, and had even ridden out to run Richards off the place. They had failed miserably and were embarrassed, some wanted out and were listening to Mel Johns, but they were afraid of being branded as cowards by a man of Harper Sloan's reputation. Others were behind Chic Took who wanted to keep on course and wipe Richards out.

Trying to get enough moisture in his mouth to speak, Johns tossed down the drink in front of him and coughed. "Mister Sloan, we've been talking about this business with Richards." His nervous hesitation was, to a man like Sloan, the same as blood to a wolf.

"You've backed out," Sloan accused with a thick sarcasm. "I've tried to make this easy for you, but now you've all turned coward and backed out leaving my men to handle this whole mess our-selves."

Chic Took's temper flared, "Not all of us have backed out! Let Johns and his weak-kneed friends belly crawl out of this, we aren't."

Sloan studied Took's bruised face, "You have a reason to fight on, don't you Chic?"

"Me and a few others intend to see Richards and McCloud dead."

"I'm glad to see someone has some guts around here."

Johns cut in, "I'm sorry, Mister Sloan, but ...."

"But ... yeah, but. But nothing! Your guts have run out plain and simple."

"We just rethought it and it's really not worth anyone getting killed over."

"I thought Chuck Sampson was a friend of yours!" Sloan was almost shouting.

A voice came from behind him, "Charlie Sampson didn't have any friends."

Spinning on his heels, Sloan came around to see a man dressed like a range rider. "Who're you?"

"Sam Raven. I manage the Juniper Cattle Company for Brian Richards. I understand you have a problem with us?"

"I have a problem with Brian Richards."

Sam Raven grinned, "Then mister, you've got a problem with all of us. We can settle this right now or deal with it later, however you want it."

"No, you're not going to bait me into anything with a room full of people. I'll deal with you later when you find out for yourself."

The grin fell from Sam's face, "Find out what?"

"That your boss is a liar and a no good cattle thief."

The punch that took Harper Sloan's feet out from under him came as unexpectedly as Sam Raven himself. He tasted the blood in his mouth as he rolled onto his knees and came back off the floor. As he did, Raven hit him again on the side of the head and put him back on the floor.

Standing over Sloan, Sam felt a blow between his shoulder blades and found himself on the floor next to him. Turning his head upward, he saw a man gripping the neck of a whiskey bottle in his hand. The blow had momentarily caused his muscles to lock up, keeping him from being able to raise his arms. The man moved at him to kick his ribs in.

As Travis Jackson was rearing back his leg to kick, a big man suddenly grabbed him from behind. With his bear-like arms around Jackson's waist, he crushed the air out of his lungs and lifted him off the ground. Confused and in pain, Jackson attempted to struggle but was powerless in the bear hug. The big man then lifted his prisoner higher and slammed him down on a table top. The scream of pain melded with the sound of crashing wood. Jackson came to a hard stop on top of the shattered table. He groaned and lay still.

The big man reached a hand down to Sam, "I told you you had a friend in Kenny Weaver."

Pulling Sam to his feet, Weaver pointed toward Sloan who was coming up off the floor. "I don't think you're done here yet."

From his knees, Sloan threw a wild roundhouse punch at Sam connecting solidly on his right hip. Wincing in pain, he stepped aside which allowed Sloan enough time to get to his feet. The two men stood toe-to-toe exchanging blows. Blood flowed from Sam's nose and his eyes were swelling. Sloan's lips were torn and his cheek bones split open. Knowing he had to finish this before his eyes were closed, Sam landed a hard right fist to Sloan's heart, dropping him in his tracks.

Breathing heavily and wiping at the blood on his face, Sam stepped back and looked down at the outlaw. Weaver bent down and examined the unconscious man. "He's alive; you just knocked all the wind out of him."

Mel Johns was on his feet staring down at Sloan, but raised his head when Sam Raven spoke, "You boys sided in with him against us, now you'll all have the devil to pay."

The men all liked Sam Raven. They respected him and had been acquainted with him, if not actual friends of his, for years. Sam looked at each of them, "Some of you were once friends of mine, but don't look for a warm welcome at my camp again. Steer clear of me from now on."

Turning slowly around Raven headed for the door, before he got out he was met by the barkeep with a wet towel. "Here, Sam, wipe your face."

Taking the towel he nodded his thanks and disappeared out the door. Standing in the sun he let the heat fall on his aching back as he tried to stretch the cramped muscles. He heard footfalls coming up behind him, realizing he wasn't in any condition to fight anymore, he pulled his gun and leveled it at the man behind him.

Recognizing Kenny Weaver he holstered the gun. "I appreciate what you did for me in there. Any time I can return the favor let me know."

"Well, funny you should say that. You happen to need a blacksmith out there on your place? If you do, I just happen to need a job."

Sam chuckled, "You know it's *funny* you should say that because a blacksmith's job just opened up."

Weaver's smile covered his broad face; the bruises received at the hands of Brian Richards were still evident. "Let me get my things and I'll ride out with you. Besides, you can use all the help you can get about now, Sloan's going to make big trouble for Richards."

Wiping the now bloody towel across his face Sam looked at the big man. "What's his game? Why is he doing this?"

"I don't know, but there's something more there than meets the eye."

"Like what?"

"I don't know, but you might want to talk to Israel about it."

"Israel Dodd? Is he in on this too?"

"He came out to Johns' place to hear what Sloan had to say, but he really told him off. He's a man on your side and he might have a few answers for you."

"Good, I've got a lot of respect for Israel; it would have been a blow to think he was my enemy now too."

"Well anyway, I'll get my gear and meet you right back here in a few minutes."

Sam nodded, "I'll be here."

As he waited and felt the sun's heat loosen his back, Sam spotted Mel Johns and the men who had once been his friends coming out of the saloon. He shouted out to them, "Mind what I said, you lousy bunch of traitors."

Mel Johns broke from the bunch and headed toward Raven. Stopping a few feet from him he searched his lost friend's battered face. "I'm sorry, Sam."

"You are that Johns, the sorriest poor excuse for a man that I care to know."

"We made a mistake Sam."

"You did that alright. What did Brian Richards ever do to any of you?"

"Well, it was about Chuck ..."

"Sampson! Who in this whole country ever gave a pinch of horse manure for Charlie Sampson? Did you?"

Johns hesitated, "No, not really. It was just that we were concerned that if a foreigner could come in here and steal one ranch, he could take everyone's."

Sam Raven's temper exploded, "No one stole anything! Sampson couldn't pay the bank what was owed because he had wiped out his range and was dead broke. He tried to kill the old Chaney woman and her daughter to steal their land and got his outfit shot to doll rags. Richards bought the note from the bank and the Marshal arrested him for trying to kill the Chaneys."

Johns stood with his mouth hanging open. "I never knew that."

"Did you ever think to ask before running off and wrongly accusing an honest man based on a pack of lies, and then starting a fight over something you were completely ignorant about?"

"I ... I don't have an answer for you Sam."

"Go home Mel. Go home and think about it."

"Are we still friends?"

Sam studied the man long and hard, "That's something I'll have to think about. For today, we're not friends any more, we'll see about tomorrow."

Turning away, Mel Johns walked slowly, his boots dragging in the sand and his head bent down. He didn't see Harper Sloan or Travis Jackson stumble out of the saloon just after he passed. He didn't hear them vow to burn the Juniper to the ground and stack the dead bodies of Richards, McCloud, and Sam Raven on top of the flames.

Chapter 8

Abby Chaney was pulling a pot of stew off the stove when Devon walked into the house. Hanging his hat on the peg next to the door, he greeted her as he lifted the coffee pot off of the stove and poured a cup. Returning the pot, he walked to the table and sat down.

"How's your morning been, Abby?"

"Oh the usual, I had high tea with the Queen of England and then came home to cook our noon meal."

Devon sipped his coffee and chuckled, "Where's Katy?"

"She went to town, said she had some business to attend to but wouldn't say what. She's been a might mysterious lately or is it my old mind playin' tricks on me?"

"She does seem to be a bit preoccupied lately, but then this trouble with that gang running wild against Brian might be bothering her."

Abby stopped moving and stared out the window. "Yeah, that sure is something alright; you think you know some folks. I guess I should rephrase that, we never really knew any of them. We were acquainted with a few while Alfred was alive, but they never showed themselves to be neighbors in any way and sure never came around to help us after he died. I don't figure to have any friends around here except Brian and his boys. The folks around here can go to blazes for all I care, them sidin' in with that slitherin' snake Sampson and all."

"Trig and Hack and I had a run-in with that Harper Sloan and his pal Jackson yesterday. Sloan was pretty cocky about it, claimed he'd fight to the last man to get Brian off that land. Jackson was pulling a gun on us under the table when Hack shoved the barrel of his Colt in his ear. You want to talk about one mighty surprised man."

Devon stopped and sipped at his coffee. "You know Abby; it just drives me crazy trying to figure out why he's so bent on running Brian out, and to the extent of killing people to do it."

"Nothin's ever the way it seems on the surface, Devon. You can bet if you back-tracked that varmint you'd find your answer."

"Well, Trig's known him for some time and he can't think of any-thing either. I guess we'll just have to wait and find out; I'm sure we will know before too long."

Before Abby could answer, the door swung open and Katy stepped inside. She was smiling and humming, carrying a bundle in her two arms. She laid the package on the table and handed Devon a letter. "This was waiting for you."

"Who would be sending me a letter?"

"Well Devon, you can try to read it through the envelope or do what most folks do and open it."

He looked up at her grinning face and then turned his eyes to-ward Abby. "Like mother, like daughter, try to get a straight an-swer." He looked back at Katy, "Your mother was with the Queen having tea again."

Katy laughed, "Oh really? Are you too good to talk to us now?"

Abby tossed her head back and stuck her nose in the air, "Maybe."

Katy looked back at Devon to find him intently reading. He looked up at her with a blank stare. "It's from my mother."

Sitting down next to him Katy's smile faded, "Is it bad?"

"Pa died over the winter, she sold the farm and is living with my sister in Wichita."

"I'm sorry about your pa, Devon."

"I guess I should have went back to see him at least once. I never went back from the time I left home at eighteen."

"But you did write, and it's a good thing you wrote at Christmas so your mother knew to find you here."

"A couple of letters over twelve years isn't much."

Katy put her hand on her husband's arm. "It's okay; mail isn't that easy to get back and forth from here. What else does she say?"

"It's not going too good for her; my sister's husband doesn't like her being there. Boy, if that don't beat all! That woman never had a cross bone in her body, how could anyone not like her?"

Abby sat down across the table from Devon, "Have her come here."

"Yeah," Katy jumped in. "They're starting a new school in town and they need a teacher, your mother would be perfect for it.

She could stay here or in town, whichever she wanted, and teach school."

Devon looked back and forth between the two women. "We could do that. I could send her the fare for the train to Boise and then a stage from there to here."

Abby stood back up, "Good, then it's settled. You get to town and send her all that. Lord knows I could use some conversation from a woman closer to my age, what with you two being off and gone all the time. Now, if there was a youngster here to make an old lady young again, well..."

"Now Ma, there you go on that again."

"If you two spent half as much time together as you do with them cows there might be one."

Katy laughed, "Well, there's going to be."

The room went silent as Abby and Devon both stared dumb-founded at Katy's announcement. Devon was the first to speak, "What you just said wasn't real clear. There's going to be one what?"

"One youngster – a baby."

Devon jumped to his feet and whooped. He grabbed his wife in a bear hug and lifted her off the floor. "Are you sure?"

"Yes, while I was in town I went to see the new Doctor, he's a very nice man by the way. I told him what I suspected and he checked and said," she lowered her voice to sound like the man, "it sure looks that way."

"When?"

"He figures the baby will come around the first of the year."

Abby's smile filled her entire face, "I guess you did get away from them cows a little bit." She threw her arms around Katy and laughed.

Stepping back Abby looked up at Devon, "Well *Pa*, that's all the more reason for you to get your mother up here. Don't want the woman missing her grandbaby. Now get on to town and send her a ticket."

Pulling his hat off the peg, he crunched it down on his head and walked out the door. The black mare was tied in front of the house, but she'd been worked pretty hard that morning and needed a rest. He led her off to the corral, stripped off the saddle and bridle and turned her in. Taking the bridle, he walked across the poled enclosure and slipped it over the head of his blue roan. Saddling the gelding, he left the corral and headed south for Drewsey.

As he rode he considered the latest events. The dirty business against Brian had just started and promised to grow worse. A gang of outlaws was behind it and men he thought were his neighbors were siding with the outlaws in an effort to destroy a man they didn't even know. He shook his head, if that didn't just beat all. The why of it still tore at him.

Then, right in the middle of it all came the letter from his mother, a complete surprise to be sure. He had had so little contact with his family over the years that they seemed almost like strangers from long ago. He felt a pang of guilt over it, but the distances of this country made it hard to do anything else. Now his father was dead and the farm he had hated as a youth sold and gone. As much as he hated that farm, he sensed a bit of sadness in its being gone, like a page of his life was thrown in the fire.

He decided that today was the start of a new time in his life. The past was gone and there was no way to change what had gone before. Today, he found out that he was going to be a father, the thought was odd and hard to grasp, but he was excited about the prospect. A man really became a man when he became a father. It didn't matter if the child was a boy or a girl, it was his child and he suddenly felt very proud.

Now, to top it off, his mother needed him and he intended to respond to that need. It reminded him of the day he woke up in the Chaney's house after being shot and left for dead by Cab Parker. He recalled how he felt when he heard that Abby and Katy were fighting alone against Taylor, Sampson, and the Parkers. He knew he needed to help them, just like now, he knew he needed to help his mother. He would talk to Morgan down at the telegraph office and see if he couldn't have a message delivered to his mother and get an answer back right away. If she wanted to come, he'd wire tickets to her for the train and stage.

His thoughts raced from one detail to the next, drifted back over the past and then would suddenly shoot ahead to the future. His mind was so preoccupied that he remembered little of the ride down the mountain until he found himself on the outskirts of Drewsey. Refocusing his attention on everything around him, he made his way to the telegraph office and dismounted.

Morgan Brainerd was seated on a stool behind the barred counter with his white sleeves bunched up with arm garters and a visor over his eyes that made his gray hair stand straight up. He looked up at the opening door. Recognizing a friend he smiled and stood up. "Devon, so good to see you, son."

"Morgan, how's it going today?"

"Just fine, just fine."

"Morgan can you send a wire to Wichita, Kansas, have it delivered, and get an answer back right away?"

"I can send the wire to the office and have it delivered, but I don't know how long that will take. I can have the person receiving the wire give an answer back to the delivery boy and they can wire that back."

"Good, let's do that."

Setting a note pad in front of him, Morgan took a pencil out from over his ear, touched the tip to his tongue and poised it over the pad. "Shoot, son."

Devon slid a strip of paper through the bars, "Here's the address." Then he began the message. "Marie McCloud. Come stay with us in Oregon. Town needs a school teacher. I'll send a train and stage ticket. Tell the delivery boy yes or no. Devon."

At the last word Morgan was tapping out the message on the key. At the end he added a request to wire him back an immediate answer. "There you go Devon, check back in an hour and we'll see if anything has come in."

"Thanks, I'll be back."

Walking back out in the street he looked up and down its length wondering what he could do for an hour or maybe even more. He wanted no part of the saloon, the last thing he needed right now was trouble. His growling stomach reminded him that he had left without eating; he decided to go to the café first.

Remounting the roan, he moved him along the street. As he passed the General Store, he recognized Trig's buckskin tied at the rail in front. He leaned down in the saddle and looked in the window and saw him standing at the counter. Swinging in next to the yellow horse, he dismounted and walked up to the store's door.

Trig's back was to him when Devon stopped just inside the room. "Parker, don't you ever go home?"

Trig spoke without turning around. "You do know that you drag your feet when you walk, don't you? Been hearing you come for the last five minutes, try picking your feet up."

Stepping up next to his friend Devon noted the items on the counter, among them were several boxes of .44 and .45 cartridges. "Going hunting?"

"Some's for Hack." Then turning his head toward Devon he added, "If I were you I'd be buying a few extra boxes too."

Devon's smile faded, "Something new turn up in all this?"

Motioning toward the door, Trig picked up his purchases and headed out with Devon right behind him. Walking to their horses they stopped next to them to talk. Trig stuffed the ammunition into his saddle bag. "Sam Raven just beat the dog snot out of Harper Sloan."

"That would have been worth seeing. What happened?"

"I just caught the tail end of it, Sloan was down on the floor and Sam was standing up. Kenny Weaver was there too."

Devon frowned, "Weaver? Whose side is he on?"

"I guess ours. Jackson tried to jump into the fight and Weaver used him to flatten a table with. Then him and Sam left together."

"That's a good sign; I'd rather have that big ox on my side than against me. Any idea what started it?"

"I asked around, it seems Sloan was calling Brian a thief and a liar. Sam heard it and the fight was on."

Devon surveyed the activity of the town around him. "It's heating up, bad blood between the Juniper and that trash of Sloan's. Any idea who around here might be siding with Sloan?"

Trig shook his head, "Not really. We know Mel Johns and that gutless wonder Farley Knolls is, and Chic Took. Who else is anyone's guess."

"I'd have expected it from Knolls and Took, and Johns isn't any brighter than he has to be. I guess we can expect it from anyone we don't know for sure to be a friend. Anyway, I was on my way to the café for something to eat; come on, I'll set you up."

"I never pass up an invite to eat." Then grinning he added, "So McCloud, don't *you* ever go home?"

"I was home, but I got a letter from my mother in Kansas. My pa died last winter and she sold the farm. We want her to come here with us, Katy says they're starting a school and could use her for a teacher. I sent a wire to Wichita and now I'm waiting around for an answer."

"I'm in no hurry; I'll wait around with you – especially if you feed me."

Shaking his head Devon laughed, "Just like a stray dog, feed him and you can't get rid of him."

"Fine, I'll leave."

"Yeah, like you'd take the chance of missing out on a good meal. Come on, let's go eat."

An hour later found the two men walking into the telegraph office. Morgan Brainerd looked up and shook his head. "Sorry Devon, nothing yet."

With a look of disappointment Devon turned to leave. Before reaching the door the telegraph key began a steady flow of code. "Hold it," Morgan shouted out, "here's your answer."

Writing with the speed of the telegraph key Morgan copied the message until the key stopped. Lifting the paper he read the message to Devon, "Marie McCloud. Yes, would love to come."

Devon quickly dug into his hip pocket and excitedly pulled out some bills. "Here, wire a train ticket to her. Can you arrange a stage ticket too?"

"I'll take care of it son; she'll be here in a week."

"Thanks Morgan. I owe you."

Morgan waved it off, "No, you don't, anything for a friend."

With a smile and a nod, Devon went out the door. Stopping in the street he waited for Trig. They both saw the riders at the same time. Trig put his hands on his hips. "Now look at that, Harper Sloan and Travis Jackson out for an afternoon ride, ain't that nice."

Sloan's battered face could be seen from a good distance and Jackson rode leaning to the left, as if favoring his right side. They were riding west, each man wearing an angry and determined expression.

Devon toed the stirrup and swung into the saddle, all the while keeping one eye on the pair of outlaws. "I wonder if it's just a coincidence that they're headed in the same direction the Juniper lays?"

"Could be, but I doubt it."

"Trig, I have to go home and let Katy and Abby know about Ma, I want you to come up with me. In the morning we'll head on down and talk to Brian."

Reining his horse around Devon pointed the roan back into town. Trig called out after him and jabbed a thumb in the direction opposite the way he was riding. "Devon, home's that-a-way."

"I know, I'm going back to the store and pick up some forty-fours."

Chapter 9

The steady drumming of Brian Richards' fingers on the walnut table by his chair was the only sound in the room. He was absorbing the account Devon and Trig had just given him regarding their encounter with Harper Sloan the day before. His fingers stopped their mechanical movement as he looked across the room at Devon.

"To the last man?"

"That's what he said." Devon's expression was that of a man who had been pushed as far as he intended to be.

Richards settled back a little more in his leather chair and grinned, "Knowing you, Devon, I'm sure you had a good reply to that."

Devon's look didn't change, "I told him that it wouldn't be him."

The grin on Brian Richards' face faded, "I can promise you he won't be."

"I'm sure you know about Sam's fight with Sloan."

"Yes, I do. He reported the fight to me as soon as he returned to the ranch. I wanted him to go back to town and see the doctor, but you know Sam. He had Kenny Weaver with him; Sam said that Kenny helped him when he was attacked from the rear."

"I saw it," Trig broke in. "Well, I saw the end of it anyway. Weaver used Sloan's pal Jackson like a pile driver and about killed him."

Richards nodded, "Sam told me. Kenny's with us now, Sam gave him a job as our blacksmith."

"He's a good one to have on our side," Devon added. "Okay Brian, any particular way you want to play this?"

"I want to keep the fight here rather than take it off the property. I warned that mob that came storming in here that the next encounter would be with guns and there would be no warnings. Let them come here and we will make a fight of it."

"I don't think that's such a good idea."

Richards turned his attention to Trig, "Why is that?"

"I know Harper Sloan and he'll backshoot your men and burn your buildings. He's a snake who'll bite without so much as a rattle. You need to take the fight to him and finish it right now."

"I understand your feelings Trig, and the manner in which you like to fight, but the law takes a dim view of what you are proposing. It could well put us in a poor defensive position if it came down to legalities."

"You won't have any legalities to worry about if you're dead and burned out."

"That is a possibility, but I prefer to keep the law on my side. It would have to be something very drastic for me to change my mind on that point."

Trig grinned, "Hear tell the Texas Rangers say to never defend when you can attack."

"They are also the law and as such have special license to attack."

With a shrug Trig stretched his legs out in front of him, "Up to you, you're the dealer here."

"Maybe, but I still appreciate your ideas and want to hear them, and I would like my friends to stand behind me."

"You think I want to miss a chance to put a bullet between Harper Sloan's eyes?"

Richards frowned, "Not if my bullet is there first."

Devon broke in, "That's exactly why we kept the shooting on the BitterGrass when we had our fight. We came out looking good and Charlie Sampson landed in prison."

Richards' frown deepened as his fingers began their drumming again. "I wonder what the motivation is behind all this. Why is this Harper Sloan so determined to run me out?"

"I've heard a couple of different things, one, that he's doing everyone in the area a favor by ridding them of a land stealing foreigner. Another is that he's avenging Charlie Sampson on principle."

Richards sniffed, "Principle? A man like that has no principles, and as Trig told us, he comes from an area south of here; why would he feel I was a threat to him? No, there is much more to this and I want to know what it is."

"I guess we'll have to wait and see what unfolds."

"Unfortunately I think you're right." Then he looked up at Trig,

"How long have you known Harper Sloan?"

"First met him about five years ago down in Reno. He had a reputation as a killer and outlaw; he had killed a few men and liked to throw his weight around."

"I know that your business is none of mine Trig, but you obviously have a grudge against Harper Sloan, what happened between the two of you? If I knew that, maybe it would shed some light on this situation."

"Sure, I can tell you. We had both been hired to oversee the interests of a mine owner in Virginia City. He was having some problems with prospectors working his claim and wanted them off by any means necessary." Trig grinned, "I'll leave that bit of the story untold. Sloan considered himself the big bull on the range and I was quite a bit younger than him, so he figured to have some sport with me and make himself look big. The short of it is, he prodded me, I braced him, and he backed down. I was younger, but I had a reputation too, so he decided not to push it. He twisted things around to make it look like he was sparing my life and I came out looking the fool instead of him. I told him then that I wouldn't be forgetting what he did and that scared him. He's still afraid of me; I saw it the other day when I ran into him, and I still intend to make him pay for that day in Virginia City."

"I can understand where the grudge comes from; I would feel the same as you. However, while you were working with him what did you learn about him or his past?"

"Not much, he was pretty tight-lipped. I know he was always partners with Travis Jackson, long before he got the rest of that pack with him. I overheard him saying something once to Jackson about a brother, but he didn't say it in a pleasant way. I took it that if he did have a brother, there was no love lost between them. That's about it, I can't think of anything that would bring him here doing all this."

Devon leaned forward in his chair and snapped his fingers in the air. "You know who might be able to give us some answers?"

A hopeful look came over Richards' face, "Who?"

"Willard Vaughn."

"Yes, I never thought of him, but he would know all about our Mister Sloan. If anyone could give us information, he could. I'll have Henry go into town and send a wire off to him today."

Trig shook his head, "I don't know about that, Brian. Henry? After what Sam just got into in town? That's a pretty rough crowd following Sloan and they're just spoilin' for a fight. You'd better send one of your tough hands, Bill Anthony would be better."

Richards chuckled, "I need Bill here to watch for invaders, besides you don't know Henry."

"They'll eat him alive and spit out his bones."

"Don't be fooled by Henry's outward appearance. He is, for certain, the perfect British gentleman; however he is also the perfect British fighter."

"Henry?"

"Henry's father served my father, as Henry serves me. Actually, let me rephrase that, Henry is my friend, confidant, and aide, he does not serve me. It is customary for a gentleman's gentleman to be followed by his son, but not so with Henry. Henry was a headstrong lad who had no desire to follow in his father's vocation. Much to his father's frustration, Henry joined the army and fought through several major campaigns and, I might add, was decorated for his bravery. While in the service of the Queen, he learned the art of bare knuckle fighting. He was actually the champion over several regiments. Later he returned home, ready to settle down and came to be in my employ. I would never trust anyone but a fighting man at my side."

Trig's mouth dropped open in amazement, "You'd never guess it by looking at him."

"That tells you how good of a fighter he was, he never endured any facial damage; he was too fast to be beaten to the punch." Richards laughed out loud, "I feel sorry for any man who thinks Henry would be an easy target to attack."

Without turning in his chair Richards raised his voice, "How many bouts did you fight Henry?"

Stepping into the room from the adjoining office, Henry spoke casually, "Thirty-seven, sir."

"How many did you win?"

"I retired undefeated, sir."

Devon smiled at Henry, "You are a man of many surprises my friend."

"It was a long time ago and now my work is here, and that is what is important." Then he turned his attention back to Richards. "How would you like the telegram to read, sir?"

"Just send it to Marshal Willard Vaughn at the U.S. Marshal's office in Baker City. Ask him to respond as soon as possible with any information he has about Harper Sloan."

"Very good sir, I will leave at once."

"And Henry, take a weapon with you."

"Yes sir, I will take the new .38."

Without another word, Henry walked to the gun cabinet and examined the firearms lying on the shelves. He picked up a Smith and Wesson .38 New Model revolver and looked it over. Checking to be sure that it was loaded, he scooped a handful of brass .38 cartridges from a paper box and dropped them in his pocket. Picking up his hat and coat he went out the door headed for the stable.

Devon watched the man with great interest. "He's a good man Brian, you're lucky to have him here with you."

Richards nodded, but his eyes showed worry for his friend. Then he returned to the previous discussion. "Do you know a man named Israel Dodd?"

"Yes I do. He's an older man, runs a few cows south of here. From what I understand he's been settled in here before anyone else came along."

"Sam mentioned him to me yesterday. He thought Mister Dodd might have some answers for us, and then Kenny told me that Dodd spoke up for us against Sloan."

"That sounds like Israel alright. No man could ever railroad him into something he was against, and the likes of Harper Sloan wouldn't scare him in the least, he's one tough old bird."

"Do either of you have any objections if we ride out to his place and talk to him?"

Devon and Trig both shook their heads. "No, let's go."

Henry's horse was just a dust cloud in the distance as Richards led his horse from the corral and saddled him. In a few minutes the three men were mounted and riding south.

Israel Dodd owned a section of good land that ran mostly to flat prairie. He ran enough stock on it to keep him in beans and beef, but not more than he could handle by himself. He had been in the area longer than most, including Charlie Sampson. He knew everyone and bowed to no one. He was a fighter and a man who never hesitated to stand on the right side of an issue.

Smoke lazily rolled out of the chimney of the old man's cabin. The three men stopped their horses short of his yard. Devon hailed the house, "Hello in the house, Israel are you in there?"

A hard gravelly voice came from the unseen interior of the cabin, "Depends. Who wants to know?"

"Devon McCloud and friends."

The door slowly opened followed by the barrel of a Winchester and then Israel Dodd. He held the rifle out in front of him as he studied the riders. "Who's that with you?"

"Trig Parker and Brian Richards."

"Brian Richards? Now, there's a man I want to meet. Any man who's got that bunch of idiots so stirred up has got to be one interestin' fellow. Step on down and come in, coffee's on the stove."

Moving their horses forward, they dismounted and followed him through the door.

Dodd nodded toward Trig. "Never liked your pa, but hear tell you're a good man." He shook Trig's hand.

Turning around, Dodd studied Richards for a moment and then stuck his hand out. "Heard a lot about you, never had the privilege though."

Richards shook Dodd's hard hand and was impressed with the old man's grip. It alone spoke volumes about the man. "Pleased to meet you, Mister Dodd."

"Israel to my friends."

With a smile Richards tipped his head forward, "Israel."

"Good, now that we've got all the formalities covered, grab a cup over yonder and pour yourself some coffee. This ain't no fancy San Francisco hotel; nobody'll be waitin' on you here."

Each man poured a cup and then looked around at the lack of chairs and politely stood holding their cups.

"Sorry about not havin' chairs, don't have much call for more'n one. I prefer being outside myself, how about you?"

Richards nodded, "I prefer talking in the fresh air as well."

Gathering under the pole roof running out in front of the cabin the men looked at Dodd. "Okay, what brings you all the way out here?"

"My manager, Sam Raven, mentioned that you might be able to shed some light on why Harper Sloan is here trying to run me out."

Dodd slurped down half his coffee and shook his head. "Don't know what it's all about. Just as much a mystery to me as to you. I went to their meeting at Mel Johns' place a while back there and listened to Sloan give his speech. The man's oilier than a St. Louie drummer. Laid out a bill of goods as to how you stole that ranch and you'd be stealin' everyone else's next. He was here to help us by gettin' rid of you and gettin' Sampson's ranch back. He went on to accusin' the three of you of bein' in cahoots together rustlin' cattle."

Devon broke in, "Which men from around here are in on this?"

"Well, there's Mel Johns. Now, there's a man with a few bricks shy of a load, dumber'n a post and twice as dense. There's Chic Took, who ain't much brighter, and that no good yella-belly Farley Knolls. He drinks too much and likes to shoot his mouth off about what a big man he is. You watch him now, nothin' sneakier than a coward with a snoot full of liquor. There's some others of no real account, just tag-a-longs. Your real problem is Sloan and his pack of coyotes."

Furrowing his brow Richards kept his eyes on Dodd's face. "Tell us about Charlie Sampson, I understand you were here when he first came."

"Yeah, I was. I recall him comin' into the area. He kept his head low and his cards close to the vest. He just showed up and started puttin' cattle on that Wire Creek range of his, and just kept puttin' 'em on until the devil wouldn't have it anymore. He was no cattleman, never was. He counted on good men like Sam and Frank Perry to keep it going, but even they couldn't do much against him. The longer he was here the nastier he got. His head swelled up and pretty soon he got to figurin' that he was the big man around here and started pushin' his weight around. He went through hands like water goes through cotton. He was just possibly the most hated man around."

"Has there ever been talk of where he came from or what he did before he came here?"

"He never allowed anyone to get close to him. I recall he had a missus at one point. Whether she came with him or he married her soon after I don't know, like I said he shied away from folks. Then somewhere along the line she got out and never came back.

What little I saw of her she seemed a decent type, not like him at all. I ain't surprised she up and left. He was almighty hard on the small settlers and the Indians, hear tell she didn't care for that none."

Pausing for a moment in deep thought, Dodd stared at the ground. "Come to think of it, I do recall hearin' a story once about a feller being in town talkin'and sayin' that Sampson was an outlaw on the dodge, but no more was ever said about that."

"Is that man still around?"

"Funny thing there, I never put it together until just now, but word had it that the man wound up dead. Shot dead out there by the river. I recall that a rumor came out that Sampson had murdered him to shut him up, but I never pay attention to rumors. Now, on recollection though, I think that just might be the facts of the matter. Charlie Sampson had a past he wanted left in the past and he was a mean one. After that no one talked about Charlie Sampson, except to cuss him for being a bad cattleman and a bad neighbor. That's why I can't see these men suddenly feelin' sorry for him. When he was here these same men hated his guts."

"That is interesting, it appears Charlie Sampson had a past and it may very well be that he is somehow connected with Harper Sloan. That would explain why Sloan is here, but not the purpose." Then putting his hand out to Dodd, Richards smiled, "Thank you for your time, we know a bit more now than we did before."

Taking his hand, Dodd smiled in return, "Don't be a stranger, come on by again."

"You do the same, Israel. Come by anytime."

Riding out of the yard the three men rode in silence, each sorting through his thoughts. There was little to discuss, they had a better idea of Charlie Sampson's past, but not any connection between him and Sloan. The only tie between them was just an unsubstantiated rumor that Sampson had an outlaw past and Harper Sloan was a known outlaw.

As the three men rode up to Richards' house, Bill Anthony came running at them from off the porch. Shouting excitedly he gasped for breath, "We've been trying to find you."

Richards pulled his horse to a stop. "We were talking to Israel Dodd. What is the problem?"

"Sam's been shot."

A flash of fear crossed Richards' face, "Where is he?"

"At the Doc's in town. He's alive, but not doing too good right now."

"What happened?"

"We don't know. A couple of the boys found him laying in the road by the north gate."

Richards looked at Devon and then to Trig, the worry etchin itself deeply into his face.

Trig shifted in the saddle and locked eyes with him. "That drastic enough for you Brian?"

The worry lines around Brian Richards' eyes suddenly changed to lines of anger. "I believe it's time I met Harper Sloan."

Chapter 10

Norm Dinton reread the telegram he had received yesterday and chuckled, he liked the way Sloan had put it. "I've got fifty reasons why you should come to Drewsey." Well, if he wanted Marshal Norman Dinton to ride all the way down there, it was going to cost him a hundred reasons. He was the big man now and his price had just doubled. He figured a hundred dollars was not unreasonable to ride over seventy miles to render his services.

Tossing the paper back on the desk, he clasped his hands behind his head and interlaced his fingers. With a smug sigh he surveyed the office around him. He had shared it with Vaughn for the two years he had been there and the old man always ran the show his way. Just because he had worked this district for over ten years didn't make him any better. Both of them were equal as deputies, but the official U.S. Marshal over at the capitol considered Vaughn the head man of eastern Oregon and treated and addressed him as U.S. Marshal rather than Deputy U.S. Marshal. That had irked him and became a sore point for the last year that he had been stuck with Vaughn. Now, by rights, he should be the big man of eastern Oregon.

He liked the feel of having the office to himself. He glanced over the wanted posters on the wall and the rifles and shotguns in the rack, the room just looked important. He was the only Federal law in these parts now and that made him the man to be reckoned with.

He never liked Willard Vaughn from the day he started; the man was always watching him as if he couldn't be trusted. Just because he took a little money now and then hardly made him a bad lawman. The pay was lousy and he had to supplement it somehow. Accepting a few bucks for services rendered was not unheard of in legal circles, so why shouldn't he?

He knew Harper Sloan had killed Vaughn, although there was no proof of it. Sloan had made it known that he was going to settle with Vaughn over the Sampson arrest. All he did was let Sloan know that Vaughn was headed for John Day and left it at that. He figured a smart man like Sloan could figure it out for himself. When neither man returned it was a simple assumption that Sloan had found him. He made no attempt to pursue the case. In fact, he never even went out to find the body, for all he knew the buzzards had finished him off. There was talk that something had happened to the Marshal, but no one knew what. Wherever the body ended up no one, as yet, had found it.

He had received a letter from the capitol wanting to know what the circumstances were surrounding Vaughn's disappearance. He grinned at the recollection of his carefully worded return answer telling how he was following every lead in an attempt to solve the case. He figured Sloan had actually done him a favor, by gunning down his arrogant partner he opened up the opportunity for him to be in charge and to prove his ability to handle the job. Then again, such information could prove valuable when the time was right. The day might come when he would need to have a little leverage over Sloan and he wasn't about to tip his hand and ruin it.

He reconsidered Sloan's request; maybe riding to Drewsey wasn't such a bad idea after all. Sloan obviously had need of his powers and was willing to pay for it, which probably meant there was an arrest to be made. Any arrest right now would make him look pretty good in the eyes of the politicians, letting them see how he was a better lawman than Vaughn. Standing up, he began to prepare for the trip. He was reaching for a Winchester on the rack when the office door opened and the telegram delivery boy ran in.

"Marshal Dinton, I've got another telegram for you. You sure are a busy man these days."

Dinton grinned with a self-satisfied tilt of his head. "Yes sir son, I'm a busy man. What do you have for me?"

"Another telegram from Drewsey."

With his face reflecting confusion, he took the paper from the boy and read it. Reading it a second time through he shook his head. He had no idea who this Brian Richards was and the fact that he had addressed the message to Willard Vaughn indicated that he had no idea that Vaughn was dead. He wanted information about Harper Sloan, and that was interesting in itself, no doubt there was a connection between the two messages.

Tossing the boy a dime, he resumed his packing as the boy scurried out the office door. Stopping, he turned and considered the two telegrams on his desk. This was something that could make him a bit of money. How much would this Richards pay for information and how much was Sloan willing to go for him not to give it? The situation presented an opportunity for him to make out pretty good all the way around.

Henry Holden was making quick time down the street walking a beeline for the doctor's office. Morgan's words pounded in his ears like the drums of a marching army, "Sure am sorry about Sam Raven being shot."

The words had hit him like a train; it was the last thing he had expected to hear. According to the old telegrapher, Sam was still alive at the doctor's, but he didn't know anything about his condition. As he approached the saloon he ignored the three men standing lazily in front of it. One was leaning on the hitchrail while the others stood slump shouldered with cigarettes hanging from their lips. He fully expected to receive their laughter, as the men around the town usually made fun of his attire. He had never spoken to any of them, choosing rather to simply ignore them.

He hoped they would mind their own business today, he was worried about Sam and not in a mood for sport. There was trouble brewing for the ranch and Brian Richards, and he could feel the gentleman in him slipping behind the soldier he had once been. It was time for fists and guns, not good manners.

Before he reached the men, he saw them focus their attention on him and begin to move his way to block him. The first man stepped in front of him with another to either side to prevent his getting past them. The man directly in front of him grinned and waited for him to stop.

Henry stopped and looked at the man with growing irritation. "Get out of my way, you fool."

With mock surprise the man laughed, "Fool? That's pretty harsh words there, fancy pants."

Henry felt the last of the gentleman slip away. "Are you part of that rabble with Harper Sloan?"

"Yeah, we ride with Harper. What of it?"

"You're boss is a pile of horse manure and so are you."

The outlaw's jaw went slack with amazement, and then he clamped his mouth shut and made a sudden move toward Henry. In a fluid move, Henry quartered his left side to the rushing man and stopped him with a solid left jab that tore his lips open. He followed it with a second and third. Stumbling back several steps, the outlaw held his hand over his bleeding lips and stared in shock.

Holding his fighting stance Henry taunted him, "Come on you gutless coward, come on in and get some more."

The man rushed in and received another jab and a right hook that dropped him in the dirt. The man to Henry's left cursed and yanked his gun out of its holster. As he was bringing the gun up level, Henry slipped the .38 out of his coat pocket and thumbed back the hammer. The shots sounded as one. The outlaw screamed out in pain and grabbed his forearm trying futilely to stop the flow of blood. His shot had gone off harmlessly in the street.

Swinging the gun around, Henry pointed it at the third man's face. "Did you shoot Sam Raven?"

The man stared in dumb silence as Henry repeated the question. "Did you shoot Sam Raven? Tell me who did or die like the cowardly dog you are."

By now a small group of men were gathering outside the saloon and more were stopping in their movements to watch the show. Some of them knew that the man holding the gun worked for Brian Richards, they had seen him going about his business from time to time and paid him little mind. He was nicknamed the *Butler* and chuckles were passed around at his dress, speech, and mannerisms, but today the laughter and jokes were directed at Sloan's men.

The man facing the rock-steady bore of Henry Holden's .38 could hear the sound of joking men behind him, but his attention was on the tightening finger around the revolver's trigger. His mind was a blur, inside of a couple of minutes one of his partners was knocked senseless and the other was down with a bullet in his arm. He knew his life now hung on the pressure of a finger.

"My patience has reached its end," Henry spoke calmly in his perfect British.

"I don't know who shot him!"

"Liar." Moving the gun slightly to the right, Henry pulled the trigger.

The man screamed in pain and panic as he slapped his hand over the blood flowing from his bullet-grazed ear. "I swear it! I really don't know, don't kill me, I don't know!"

"Where's Harper Sloan?"

"Haven't seen him all day."

Henry shifted the bore to the man's opposite ear. "Want a matching set?"

The outlaw instinctively covered his other ear. "No! I haven't seen him. He's been gone since yesterday, right after he had the fight with Raven; him and Jackson both. For God's sake mister, don't shoot!"

Considering the man's terror-filled pleas, Henry decided that he was telling the truth. The outlaw let out a loud sigh of relief as Henry lowered the gun; his muscles suddenly relaxed causing him to slump forward.

"When you do see that cringing hyena, tell him that we will be looking for him."

As if he never stopped, Henry resumed his rapid pace bound for the doctor's house. The outlaw stood in the street holding a bloody hand over his ear, refusing to look at the crowd of men laughing at him. He staggered away, leaving his wounded partner sitting in the street and the other groggily working himself up to a standing position on two shaky legs.

Marching up the walk to the doctor's door Henry stopped and rapidly knocked several times on it. Immediately the door swung open and a stern faced man of fifty eyed him. His angry brown eyes began to soften as he took in the cut of Henry Holden.

"I am terribly sorry, Doctor, for rapping on your door in such an angry manner. I've just had a violent confrontation with three of Harper Sloan's thugs and I am a bit excited."

Doctor Peter James couldn't stop the grin that played at the corners of his mouth. The man's British accent and perfect speech were a pleasant change from the rough language of the country he was accustomed to. "That's quite alright sir, I am well aware of the problems caused by the outlaws of our town. How can I help you?"

"I am from the Juniper Cattle Company and I understand you have one of our men who was shot today. I am here to see as to his welfare."

The grin disappeared from the doctor's lips. "Oh yes, I have Sam Raven in here. Come on in."

Sweeping his hat off his head, Henry entered the room with the doctor closing the door behind him. Gripping the hat nervously in his two hands, Henry twisted the brim. "What is his condition?"

"He's tough and holding his own, but he took a bullet in the chest. I did what I could for him and got the bullet out, now it's all between him and the Good Lord."

"He may die then?"

"He may. He's hit hard enough and has a hole in his lung, but like I said he's a tough man, he might pull through. However, even if he does he'll be a long time recovering; a lung doesn't heal very fast."

"Is he unconscious?"

"Yes, has been since his friends brought him in here."

"Then it would serve no purpose to see him."

"You're welcome to, but he won't know it."

"Very well then, my time would be better served hunting down his assassin than to stand here. Thank you for your time and care of Sam."

"I wish I could be more encouraging."

Henry bowed slightly and turned on his heel for the door. "Thank you all the same."

Unlike the local cowhands who never walked when they could ride, Henry enjoyed walking. He had left his horse tied in front of the telegraph office and walked to the doctor's, now he retraced his steps. Passing the spot where his confrontation with the outlaws had taken place, he found the three men gone along with the crowd of watchers. He walked with the determination of a man bent on a mission. Men he passed stopped and looked at him, this time with respect in their eyes rather than humor. The *Butler* had earned his place on the high desert.

Half way back to the house Henry encountered Brian, Devon, and Trig riding hard for town. They pulled up when they came to him.

Richard's face was set in stone. "Henry, did you hear about Sam?"

"The telegrapher told me and I went to the doctor's to see to his condition. He is not doing well; he was shot through the lung. The doctor said he has done all he can for now."

Richards cringed, "Will he live?"

"The doctor was unsure; he could go either way at this point."

"Did you get the telegram off?"

"Yes, and to answer your next question, Harper Sloan is not in town, I asked as to his whereabouts and was told he was not anywhere to be found."

"Well, we'll see about that. I intend to find him and put an end to this right here and now."

"I will return to the house and see to matters there."

"Very well, we will continue on to town."

Putting heels to his horse Richards moved him forward. Without looking back, he spoke as if to himself, "I can tell by Henry's eyes that he had trouble in town. We will find out what manner of it when we get there."

The three men rode the length of Drewsey's main street looking for horses that would match Sloan's or his friends. Finding nothing in particular, they returned to the saloon and dismounted. Richards was the first one through the door.

Stopping just inside, the three men scanned the crowd and recognized only a few locals. The barkeep came from around the end of the bar and approached them. "We heard about Sam, he's got a lot of friends pulling for him. Any idea who shot him?"

Richards turned slightly to face the man, "I was hoping you could tell me. I understand he had a fight in here yesterday with Harper Sloan."

The barkeep vigorously nodded his head, "Yep, he sure did. Just beat the hell out of him." His expression suddenly turned to that of a man who had just answered his own question. "I'll bet a dollar to a biscuit that Sloan either did it, or at least was behind it."

"No bet my friend, I know he did it and I intend to put an end to him."

"I haven't seen him since that fight," then starting to chuckle he broke into a roar of laughter. "Your man was here earlier, you know, the *Butler*."

Richards gave the man an angry glare, "He's not a *butler!*"

"I know, I know, but the boys call him that. It's okay. After today, he's a respected man around here."

"What happened today?"

The barkeep could hardly speak clearly for laughing. "Three of Sloan's monkeys tried to have some fun with him."

"Are they still alive?"

"Barely, he beat one senseless and shot the other two."

Richards cast a quick glance at Trig who was listening with a slack jaw. "Henry can take care of himself."

"You're telling me! That show was worth buying a ticket for."

The conversation came to sudden close as the loud commotion of drunken voices coming in the saloon took their attention. The three men turned together to see Farley Knolls, Chic Took, and another local Sloan supporter coming in. They stopped up short, turning instantly silent at the sight of the men in front of them.

Chic Took's eyes locked on Devon and he began to back out the door. Knolls was drunk enough not to recognize the danger and he pushed it.

"Well, if it ain't the Juniper cattle rustlers, come to see about your man? Ol' Sam's not so tough now is he?"

Without a word, Richards jumped forward landing both his open hands on Knolls' chest. Driving hard with his weight behind him, he shoved the drunken man back out the door. Knolls hit the packed street hard on his back, the wind blowing out of his lungs.

Digging deep for a breath, he managed to draw his lungs full and stagger up to his feet. As he did his gun was coming clear of the holster, clumsily he lifted it all the while keeping his eyes on the man who had knocked him down. He had had enough of Brian Richards.

Seeing the move, Richards' hand dropped down on the butt of the Thunderer and smoothly brought it forward. The Colt's double action saved Richards the second that Knolls needed to thumb back the hammer of his .45. Knolls' eyes widened in terror as he watched the hammer of Richards' gun pull back and snap forward. The bullet hit him hard in the chest hurtling him backwards.

The smell of the burnt powder lingered momentarily before disappearing on the breeze. Chic Took stood frozen in place as his liquor-soaked mind came to realize that Farley Knolls was lying dead in the street. He slowly looked up at Richards.

Moving the gun toward Took, Richards spoke calmly, "You go tell your Master Sloan that I am looking for him, he wanted a fight and now he has one. He drew first blood on one of my men, now one of yours is dead; there will be no mercy from me, I intend to kill you all. You tell him Brian Richards has come out to fight."

Chapter 11

Drewsey was still a good hour away when Norm Dinton cleared a curve in the road and came face-to-face with two men on horseback. He pulled up and looked at them. "Okay Harper, I got your message, what's going on?"

Sloan gave the marshal a mock smile, "What, no hello? Old friends like us and no hello? I have to say Norm, I'm hurt."

"You'll get over it. Got the money?"

"Fifty dollars."

"No, it's a hundred dollars Harper."

Sloan's face went sour. "Getting greedy on us, Norm?"

"Nope, just business. I'm the head man now and my price went up." Then with a look of false concern he added, "You did hear that some villain gunned down poor Willard Vaughn, didn't you?"

"I heard something about him disappearing and nobody knows where he went."

"Well *I know,* and now you understand why my price went up."

Sloan shrugged his shoulders, "Why tell me? Why should I care?"

"Oh, because you were making noise around Baker City that you were going to get Vaughn and now he's dead. I can do that arithmetic in my head and two-plus-two comes up to four pretty darn quick. So, it's a hundred bucks or I go back to Baker."

"Well Norm, you'd have a hard time making that one stick, and then again, you were the one who told me that Vaughn was heading for John Day. A suspicious person could say you had a hand in the marshal's death. Seems we're about even on that one, but, I'll tell you what, I'll give you the hundred because I need you to do something very important for me."

"What is it?"

"Pretty simple really, just arrest two cattle thieves and take them back to Baker City with you."

"What's so special about these two that you'd call me all the way down here to arrest a couple of cattle thieves when the whole country is crawling with them?"

"Let's just say they're in the way of my completing my business here."

"Why don't you just shoot them?"

"Because I want this to look all legal and right. When my business is done what they do won't matter; you can release them and all is well. If they're dead there's too much explaining to do."

Dinton considered the situation. "Sounds easy enough. Where do I find them?"

"We'll help you with that, but first you need to deputize Travis and me to help make sure they get behind bars and out of this country. We'll help you get them to Baker City and then we'll come back here to finish up."

"Got the hundred?"

Flipping up the flap of his saddlebag, Sloan fished out several bills and handed them to Dinton.

Dinton's eyes lit up with greed and satisfaction as he accepted the money and put it in his shirt pocket. "Okay, raise your right hands."

Both outlaws raised their hands. "Do you swear to be loyal deputies to the United States Marshal?"

Both men answered together, "I do."

"There you go, you're my deputies. Now, let's go find your cattle thieves."

"Come on Norm, we know where to find them; they've got bordering places up in the hills here. We can catch them while they're out working."

The bruises on Sloan's face had not escaped Dinton's notice. "Your face have anything to do with these two men we're going after?"

"Naw, them and this," Sloan pointed to his face, "have nothing to do with each other. One's been dealt with, the other is soon to be."

Dinton fell silent and let his horse follow Sloan and Jackson up into the hills. The open country gradually gave way to stands of Lodgepole and Ponderosa pine. They rode on through the timber until they came out into a wide expanse of good pasture. Scattered across the landscape were clusters of cattle.

Sloan reined back on his horse and stopped at the tree line.

Tipping his jaw up he indicated the country ahead of them. This here's the land one of them owns; over that way is his friend's."

Looking the place over Dinton pointed to the cattle, "Those your rustled stock?"

"Not mine – a friend's. I want to see justice done on his behalf."

Dinton hissed, "As if you cared about anyone but yourself."

Sloan gave him a cold glare, "I care about this one."

With a shrug Dinton looked back at him, "All the same to me, just point them out."

"There's a road to the south here that seems to be their way in and out. We'll head down that way and wait for a while."

Finding a long stretch of open road where they could watch both directions while staying concealed in a cluster of brush and pine, they settled in and watched. The afternoon dragged on slowly with no sign of riders. Norm Dinton was not a patient man and the waiting was becoming stressful. To Sloan and Jackson it was all part of the game, they had waited many an hour for a stage to come by.

Dinton stood up and stretched his legs. "You might as well tell me why I'm arresting these men and what their names are. It might prove embarrassing if I'm asked about it and I have no answers."

Sloan looked up at the marshal from his seat in the sand. "Man's name is Devon McCloud; he helped steal Chuck Sampson's cattle."

"How do you know that?"

"Because he has the animals on his property with Sampson's brand."

"Maybe he bought them."

"Norm, do you want the hundred or do you want to give it back to me and you can go home?"

"Just trying to get my answers straight."

"Just arrest McCloud and his pal, okay?"

"How do you know they're coming? You been to town lately to find out what's going on?"

Sloan shook his head in irritation, "They have to come this way. There's plenty going on right now to draw them into town, and no we haven't been to town in three days. We've been out here waiting for you to finally show up. Any more questions? You sound like a school teacher."

Stretching his neck up, Dinton stared down the road toward Drewsey. "Just one, is that them coming up the road?"

Sloan jumped to his feet and stared down the road. "Yep, that's them. Get on your horses and get ready. Travis, you get behind them and Norm and I will stop them from the front."

Mounting their horses, the men moved behind the pines and made ready to spring the trap. As Devon and Trig came up alongside the hiding place, Dinton and Sloan kicked their horses out in front of them. Pulling to a stop, they blocked the road with their guns drawn while Jackson came out behind them.

Trig turned his head slightly to look at Jackson and then looked back at Sloan.

"Get out of the way Sloan before I clear that saddle of yours."

Dinton moved his horse forward and pulled back his vest to reveal his badge. "Just a minute there mister, U.S. Marshal Norm Dinton here, which one of you is Devon McCloud?"

Devon eyed the marshal and then locked eyes with Sloan.

Sloan's eyes danced with triumph. Pointing at Devon he answered, "That one, Marshal."

Studying Devon for a moment he looked back at Trig. "What's your name?"

"Trig Parker – why?"

At the name Dinton shot a dirty look at Sloan and then lifted his Colt to cover both men in front of him. "You're both under arrest for cattle theft."

"What?" Devon snapped back at him. "Cattle theft! On whose word – his?" He pointed at Sloan.

"You're going back with me and my deputies to Baker City until we sort this business out. I suggest you go along peacefully and get there alive."

Trig burst out laughing, "Deputies! Them two outlaws? I can see what kind of lawman you are."

Devon eyed the marshal with a cold glare. "I thought Willard Vaughn was the marshal in this district?"

"*Was,* McCloud, you were right on that one. Marshal Vaughn was killed in the line of duty a couple weeks back. I'm the man to deal with now."

Devon nodded, "I can see where all this came from. How much

did Sloan pay you?"

Trig broke in, "Doesn't matter, we're not going."

Dinton thumbed back the hammer of his revolver, "Over your saddle or sitting up in it, but you're going."

"Not if I kill you first."

"Hold it Trig," Devon stopped him, "they'll kill us both before we can get our guns out and then they *will* have an easy run of it."

Dinton grinned, "Better listen to your friend, besides it'll go a lot worse for you if you draw on a United States Marshal. Right now you're just looking at theft, don't make it worse."

"We'll go with them Trig and fight this thing." Then looking back at Dinton, "Can I go tell my wife?"

"No, I think that would be a bad idea. The fewer people who know ,the better. Now, pull them six-guns out with your thumb and finger and drop them."

Trig looked anxiously at Devon, whose quiet manner and knowing nod indicated that they would work through this. Slowly they lifted their guns out of the holsters and dropped them in the road.

"Very good boys. Now if you promise to behave I won't tie you up; but if I have any problems with you, you'll look like a rope factory. What'll it be?"

Devon moved his horse forward, "Fine, let's just go."

Dinton took the lead, with Sloan and Jackson bringing up the rear behind Devon and Trig. They turned east with the setting sun behind them.

Katy McCloud paced nervously across the cabin floor. Every few minutes she opened the door and stepped out on the porch and listened. The setting sun was casting long shadows across the grass as she wrapped her arms around her belly and tried to feel her baby.

Abby quietly stepped up next to her and watched the sun steadily sinking behind the ridge. "He's probably just been delayed. Maybe Sam's doin' better and they stayed with him a while longer."

Katy shook her head, "I don't think so. They were due back this afternoon and with all the trouble going on right now Devon knows I would be worried if he did that. No, something happened to him."

"He's with Trig; do you think those coyotes could take both of them tough men?"

"Sam is a tough man too and now he's hanging on by a thread with a bullet hole in his chest."

The two women stood together in silence and listened. Katy strained her ears, willing the sound of horses to come through the growing darkness, but nothing came, only the wind in the trees.

Turning briskly back into the house she grabbed for her hat and coat. "I'm heading down the road to see."

Putting a gentling hand on her daughter's arm Abby looked in her eyes, "You can't find anything in the dark, and if there is a sign you'll ride right past it or worse, over it. There's more than you to think about now. What would Devon tell you to do?"

Dropping the coat on the floor, Katy wiped a tear out of her eye. "He'd say wait here."

"We'll keep a lamp turned low in the window for him and if he's not back come morning then we'll take the wagon and go lookin'."

Katy nodded and slowly walked to a chair and sat down. "You go on to bed Ma, I'm not sleepy."

Pulling back the curtain from the window, Abby turned the oil lamp down low and placed it on the sill letting its glow cast out into the dark. Turning, she walked past Katy, patted her shoulder and went off to bed.

Sitting in the chair, Katy continued to listen. She laid her hands on her stomach and wished the baby was big enough to bulge her belly and move. Staring at the dull light inside the lamp's chimney, she thought over the last year with Devon.

She vividly saw the day when her mother had brought him into the house all covered in blood. Little had she known then what her mother's act of kindness would do for them. In spite of how she felt, she couldn't stifle the growing grin when she recalled asking Devon if he *had any sand.* He stayed and fought their war against Sampson and Taylor, even though it wasn't his fight. If not for Devon, they'd be long dead and the ranch gone. Now she waited for him to come home, with another war brewing and men being shot. Something had happened to him, she knew it and the tears began to flow without stopping.

The feeling of a hand on her shoulder stirred her awake, she jerked her head up and shouted, "Devon."

"No honey it's just me, you slept in that chair all night."

Feeling the disappointment overwhelm her Katy looked past the lamp that was now out, and into the sunlit world. Standing up slowly, she let her stiff muscles stretch until she could walk. "I'm going after Devon."

"I've got the wagon hitched, let's both go down the road and see what we can find."

Leaving the house, they climbed into the wagon and moved the team out of the yard and onto the road. Katy watched in every direction as they moved along trying desperately to not miss anything that could give them a clue as to Devon's disappearance.

After a mile had been put behind them with no indication of trouble, Katy began to relax and hope that Devon and Trig had stayed in town with Sam. Maybe they never came up here at all; maybe she was just imagining trouble where none existed. She began to feel a little relief, then a touch of anger that her husband would put her through this anxiety. She would have to have a word with him about that.

They were just reaching the southern boundary of their property when Abby pulled back on the reins and stopped the team. Katy was looking off to her right when she felt the wagon stop; instinctively she jerked her head around to look at her mother, and then followed her gaze down to the road bed.

At first she didn't see what Abby was looking at and then the objects jumped into focus. Fear gripped her throat as she leaped from the wagon seat and ran up the road. Stopping over the objects she froze in place, and then as if in a trance she reached down and picked up the two guns. She held them up and faced her mother.

Walking back to the wagon Katy looked up. "It's Devon's."

"And Trig's," Abby added. "It takes something unusual for a Parker to give up his gun."

Katy shook her head, "I don't understand, what does this mean?"

Abby pointed at the side of the road. "For one thing, that trail was left by several riders, which means they were took off from here. This also means they're not dead and that's something to be thankful for."

"Maybe, but not knowing what happened to them is frightening in itself." Katy walked around the wagon and climbed up to her seat. "But I guess there's hope."

"I recall another time when we thought there was no hope," Abby offered a comforting smile.

Katy's eyes suddenly opened wide, "Oh my gosh, I just remembered, Devon's mother will be at the stage station tomorrow. Devon was going to meet her."

"Well, we'll just have to meet her ourselves, but right now we need some help." Moving the team forward she added, "We need Brian."

The echoing hooves of a hard running horse caused both women to suddenly jerk around to see who was coming down the road behind them. The road they had just traveled over had a low spot that now hid the horseman, but they could hear him coming. As they watched, Hack Parker blasted over the rise at a full gallop. He saw the wagon blocking his route and began pulling the horse up. Bringing the horse down to a walk he made his way to the wagon.

"Aunt Abby, Katy, what are you doin' out here?"

Abby pointed at the lathered horse, "What are you doin' runnin' that horse to death? Where's the fire?"

"Trig never came back from town and I'm going to find out why. I'm sure Sloan's outfit did something to him and if they did, I'm going to kill the whole pack of 'em."

Katy held up the two Colts, "We came looking for Devon, he never came home either."

Hack's eyes focused on the guns in his cousin's hands and then filled with recognition. "That's Trig's .45, where did you get it?"

"They were both lying in the road right here."

Rage began to fill the young man's face. "That cinches it; Trig would never just drop his gun." He began to kick his horse forward when Abby stopped him.

"Hold up Hack, there's a trail heading east from here made by several riders and we think Devon and Trig got took off from here."

"Took off? Trig would never let the likes of Harper Sloan just *take* him off anywhere. I don't believe that."

"Devon wouldn't either, but for some reason they both dropped their guns and rode off with those others."

Hack frowned, "The only way them two would do that is if it was the law. Why would the law want them? Trig hasn't been in any trouble for over a year and Devon never was."

"Besides," Katy broke in, "Willard Vaughn is the law around here and he knows Devon. He would never take him away without telling us and what would he take him away for? No lawman in his right mind would believe that nonsense about our stealing Sampson's cattle, it's too easy to prove our ownership."

"I don't know, but I intend to follow that trail until I find an answer. Trig knows I'll come after him and he'll leave me signs."

Abby nodded, "That's a good idea. You follow that trail and we're headin' down to see Brian and get some help from him."

Hack held out his hand. "Let me have those guns. When I find Trig and Devon, they'll want them."

Katy handed him the guns and watched as he put them in his saddlebags. Reining his horse off the road, Hack struck the trail and shouted back over his shoulder, "I'll find 'em and bring 'em back, or die in doin' it."

Chapter 12

Abby and Katy sat on the wagon seat in silence; Abby held the reins snug as the horses wanted to move faster than either of them cared for on the bumpy road. They were worried about Devon and Trig and just as worried about meeting Devon's mother without Devon. What would the woman think? What could they tell her about the fight and Devon's disappearance? They hoped she was as tough as her son.

Beside them, Brian Richards rode in equal silence. Their message of the mysterious disappearance of his friends had disturbed him beyond words. It was possible that such a thing could happen to one of them, but to both was too strange to comprehend. Two men who had the fighting abilities of Devon and Trig didn't just drop their guns and disappear, something happened to them, something bad.

With all of the violence that had taken place in the past days, the three of them all feared for the worse. Richards felt personally responsible and anguished over the expectant young wife losing her husband on his account, the thought was unbearable. He had expressed as much to Abby and had received her rebuke for it; she had called it 'foolish talk.'

Abby knew how he felt and didn't want the silence between them to seem like anger. "We sure appreciate your ridin' with us Brian and you with so much to do."

Thankful for the break in the silence, he smiled weakly. "It is the least I could do. With all this trouble going on I would never leave you to ride all the way to Buchanan by yourselves."

The women had not missed that Brian now carried a rifle on his saddle along with his revolver. He was leaving nothing to chance and was ready to fight at all times.

Katy looked toward him, "Yes Brian, thank you. I feel safer with you along."

"I have seen the two of you fight. I'm not your protector, just simply one more gun."

The three turned to silence once again, they were not people given to small talk strictly for the sake of saying something. Katy could stand the awkwardness no longer. Looking past her mother she centered her attention on Brian. "Brian, Ma told me what you said last night."

Richards was slightly taken aback by the statement, he had not wanted Katy to hear his fears for her and her husband. Then again, he wasn't surprised in light of the fact that this concerned all of them and mother and daughter were very close.

"I know how badly you feel, but don't! If it wasn't for you, we would all be dead right now and none of this would be taking place at all. Sampson had us all down and shot up with only a couple of cartridges left between us when you showed up, it was like a miracle. Now, you have a problem and I'll be damned if you think we are going to just stand by and watch! Devon's a fighting man, so is Trig, and wherever they are they *will* come out on top. We are all in this fight together because that's what friends are for. Now you just get that foolish idea of making me a widow out of your head!"

Richards' jaw went slack as he listened to the scolding from the young woman. It was much like the one he received from her mother the evening before. He had never heard Katy raise her voice or swear, to do so meant she was adamant about what she said. It was obvious she was made up of the same steel as her mother and father.

Searching for the right words, Richards stared at Katy. Abby turned her head slightly and gave him a knowing look. "Told you Brian. Now, let's get our attention on the tasks at hand and stop whippin' ourselves."

Richards nodded his head. "I believe I have been told all right . . . twice. I will respect your wishes and consider this matter another element we must overcome. Besides, Hack is on their trail and an outstanding young man he is too."

In an effort to change the subject, he considered what kind of young man Hack Parker was. "Interesting young man that Hack. No education, cannot read or write above a child's level, yet he is incredibly wise and intelligent."

"Education is a fine thing Brian."Abby continued to study the road in front of her, "But folks have an idea that unless you've sat in a schoolroom and learned from a school teacher, a person can't be intelligent. Nothing personal Brian, but some of the biggest fools I've ever met were well educated in books and such, and some of the wisest never set foot in a school room. Hack needs to learn to read and write because the world is changing, and if he can't read and write then he's going to have some problems. On the other hand, Hack soaked in every livin' thing around him and learned from it. Right now, if I had my choice between Hack on those boys' trail or some dude with a full blown education, well, give me that backwoods boy."

"I have to agree with you Abby; in my travels I have met both as well. I have met people who were actually so overeducated that they could do nothing of value because all their time had been spent studying theory and never applying it to life. On the other hand, I've known simple people who had the wisdom of Solomon. I have also known the opposite. Those whose education served them well and made a good person better, and the ignorant of the world that cared little for bettering themselves and chose to live in ignorance."

"Amen!" Abby nodded her head, "We all need to see each man and woman for what they are, not how they appear."

The education discussion ended, but it brought a feeling of peace over them. The heavy silence and fear had lifted and the friends were once again open to each other. The blame rested squarely on the shoulders of Harper Sloan and not them. If not for Sloan none of these problems would be on them today. Eliminating Sloan would put an end to the whole affair.

As the team strained against the harness to pull the wagon up the hill, the building that constituted the Buchanan Stage Stop came into view. The square-topped span of rim rock behind it was the natural marker all riders looked for in approaching the stop, an indication that their journey was nearing its end.

Topping out on the hill, they pulled the wagon to the side and the two women climbed off the seat. Abby forced her stiff muscles to move and little-by-little, eased her way to the ground. She was a proud woman and Richards knew better than to try to assist her. He had learned that lesson the hard way, if Abby Chaney wanted help she would ask for it.

Standing in the stirrups, Richards searched down the desert road for the dust cloud that would signal the arrival of the stage. Far off in the distance he spotted a plume of dust rising into the sky indicating that the stage was somewhere under it. "I see the stage coming or at least its dust."

Abby slapped at the coat of dust that clung to her, "Good, we won't have long to wait."

Katy clasped her hands together in front of her, she was nervous about meeting Devon's mother, especially under these circumstances. She had no idea what to tell her except the truth. She dropped her hands to her sides and stared down the road.

Another twenty minutes passed before the sound of horses' hooves, slapping leather, and rattling wood came up the hill to them. The stage topped the hill with the driver pulling back on the reins and applying the brake with his foot. They could make out two passengers inside the coach and then it came to a stop, with the coach rocking back and forth on its springs.

Jumping down from his place, the driver opened the coach's door and held it open. A woman bent forward and made her way out, with the driver holding her hand she worked her way down the steps. "This is it Mrs. McCloud, looks like your folks are here to meet you."

She gave the man a warm smile. "Thank you Mister Kent, you have been very kind."

The driver returned the smile and tipped his hat. A man came out behind her; he and the driver walked behind the stage and unbuckled the luggage compartment. He then lifted a small chest and a large carpet bag out and placed them on the ground. The two men turned and walked into the building.

Making their way toward her, Abby and Katy were surprised to find that Marie McCloud was younger than they had expected her to be. They had foreseen her as older and gray haired, as it was, she was at the most fifty and her black hair had only now begun to show streaks of gray.

Richards was the most surprised, he was instantly taken with the woman's fine features. He could very well see the French in her dark eyes and hair, and she was only slightly younger than him. He moved toward her following the women.

Thrusting her hand out Abby smiled. "Abby Chaney, mighty pleased to meet you." She was not surprised to find Marie's hand to be firm and calloused.

Marie was not taken aback by Abby's gruff appearance and speech; she was also a farm woman from the wilds of the Kansas prairie. "Thank you Abby, it's a pleasure to meet you too."

Looking past Abby, Marie turned her attention to Katy, but as she did her eyes passed over Brian and lingered perhaps a second longer than was proper. Breaking her eyes off the man she focused on Katy. Reaching out her arms she embraced the young woman. "Of course you are Katy."

Katy returned the hug. "I am so happy to finally meet you. Devon has told us so much about you that we feel you have been here all along."

Marie smiled warm and loving. "I have heard so little from my son over these past years, but his last letter told me all about you."

Brian hung politely back while the women got acquainted. Marie once again cast a curious glance his way, the look was caught by Katy. Turning slightly toward Brian she smiled, "This is our very good friend, Brian Richards."

Marie watched him as he stepped forward. Smiling she held her hand out. "A pleasure to meet you as well."

Brian bowed slightly, "The pleasure is all mine."

The strong British accent froze Marie McCloud in mid-movement. Her smile turned stiff, as her hand stopped its forward motion. Brian instantly realized the awkwardness of the moment. He recalled the talks he and Devon had had concerning the feelings his family held toward the British. Devon's father had been staunch in his hatred of everything English, but his mother was a fairer person.

Marie forced her smile to widen and moved her hand forward to take Brian's. "Mister Richards."

Taking her hand briefly he smiled, "Mrs. McCloud."

She held his eyes briefly, her own reflecting confusion. A lifetime of strong feelings and practiced beliefs were running into the reality that Brian Richards did not match any of it. He was obviously kind and well mannered and not prejudiced toward her Acadian blood or her son's for that matter. She suddenly felt a flash of shame for having such a reaction to the man.

In an effort to cover her reaction she laughed lightly, "Mister Richards, your accent surprised me, are you English?"

Richards knew the source of the question. "Yes, I am." In an effort to let her know that he understood how she felt he added, "Devon and I have spoken much about our ideas. I understand how you feel; I only trust that you will allow me to dispel your feelings about my nationality. Devon and I are good friends, I hope we can be as well."

"Perhaps." This time her smile was genuine.

Abby and Katy watched the brief exchange with interest. At first there was a wave of fear that there was going to be bad blood right off. Then, the two became friendly and a twinkle of amusement lit in Abby's eyes. She and Katy exchanged sly grins.

Marie then turned her attention back to Katy and Abby. "Speaking of Devon, is he here? Didn't he come with you?"

The amused grins quickly disappeared. Abby gestured for them to walk to the wagon where they could talk. Brian picked up the chest and Katy took the bag. With a deep sigh, she began to explain to Marie what had taken place since her son had been found shot and left for dead on her ranch. She briefly described the fight with Sampson and the parts Devon, and then Brian, played in their rescue. She then went on in more detail about the present situation with Brian, ending with Devon and Trig's disappearance. In the ensuing silence they held their breath waiting for Marie's response.

Marie stood silent, the look of shock and fear they had expected never came. She looked off toward the rim rock above them and then returned her gaze to the three. "Devon is the image of his father; Enos would never walk by when another needed help. He was quick to fight, especially an injustice. I would expect nothing less from my son."

Then turning her head slightly she looked directly at Brian. "My son must regard you very highly to risk his life for you, and that is no small thing Mister Richards. Then of course, you have done the same thing yourself."

Looking back at Katy she added, "He *will* be home."

The answer held them all in silence; they had envisioned everything except this courageous reaction to their story. Abby immediately felt pride in the woman and a bond started to grow between them. They were the same kind of women. Katy was relieved that what she had feared so much was now resolved.

A glow came on the young woman's face. "I was so worried about how we were ever going to explain Devon's disappearance to you. We are all very worried about him, but like you, we know he will be home."

"Of course he will," Abby broke in. "He's tougher'n whale bone."

Marie smiled, "I take it you like my son?"

"Like him! If it weren't for Devon we'd both be dead now. Then he goes and makes a first rate son-in-law on top of it. Yeah, I like him."

"You're fortunate," Marie's smile faded. "My son-in-law doesn't like me."

Abby nodded, "I heard. I also understand you lost your husband over the winter."

"Yes, he took the fever and never came out of it."

Abby gave her an understanding look, "I lost my man some time back, it was hard, but we've moved on ahead of it."

"I have as well. We're not a people given long to grief, we move on. I sold the farm; I didn't really want to stay on it without Enos. The money has provided me some security."

Abby took her new friend's hand, "Well, we're all kin here and family is everything to us. You're welcome with us for as long as you like."

Marie put her free hand on Abby's, "Thank you, I feel at home already."

Katy peered up at the sun as it began to arch to the west. "I think we had better be heading back if we want to be home before dark."

Abby climbed up in the driver's seat of the wagon. Katy gestured toward the open seat, "Mrs. McCloud you sit up on top, I'll ride in the back."

"Honey, you can't be calling me Mrs. McCloud. Lands sakes, you're my daughter. Call me Ma."

Katy hesitated looking up at her mother for approval. She felt strange calling another woman Ma. Abby laughed, "You're one lucky girl, you've got two Ma's."

"Okay Ma, you sit up there with Ma and I'll sit in the back." Picking up the bag, Katy climbed into the back of the wagon and sat next to the chest. Picking up the rifle, she laid it across her legs and began watching the country around them.

Marie laughed as she made her way to the opposite side of the wagon. She took hold of the board sides preparing to climb up when she felt a strong hand support her arm. She glanced sideways to see Brian standing at her side. She hesitated for a moment while looking at him.

"May I assist you, Mrs. McCloud?"

Another silent second passed then Marie smiled, "Thank you, Mister Richards."

Supporting her until she was safely on the wagon seat, Brian then turned and walked to his horse. Pulling the reins loose he toed the stirrup to mount. Abby leaned over to Marie and whispered, "He was my Alfred's best friend and a mighty fine man."

Marie watched him as he smoothly mounted and reined his horse around. The same debate raged in her mind as it had in Devon's over a year ago. He was the hated English, but yet he was different. She nodded, "Yes, he does seem to be."

Chapter 13

The funeral for Farley Knolls was a quick one. The Undertaker had refused to bury him since there was no one to pay the expenses and no one was willing to volunteer their backs to dig the hole. The body had laid in a livery stall for over a day before the hostler got tired of looking at him and did the job himself. Most men around Drewsey could care less that one more outlaw had been planted with a couple ounces of lead in his body, it was just business as usual.

Wrapped in a blanket, his body was unceremoniously dropped in a shallow grave. The only ones who watched the burying were Chic Took and five others who had sided with Knolls; Mel Johns was not among them.

The hostler gave the men a disgusted look. "There, I dug the hole, you want him buried you do it." He threw the shovel down at their feet and walked away.

Chic Took picked up the shovel and began tossing shovelfuls of dirt in the hole. As the blanket disappeared under the growing mound of dirt Took looked up at the men with him. "Who's with me to ride on Richards and kill him?"

All five men voiced an angry oath to avenge Farley Knolls. Earl Felts spit on the ground and slapped his hand down on his holstered gun. "Let's do it. I think this whole thing has gone on long enough; first Chuck and now Farley."

"Don't forget about me," Took growled, "I got a beating out of this myself."

"That's right," another voiced chimed in, "Chic got it from that bunch, too. The time has come to take back our country from that thieving, murdering outfit."

A tall, rail-thin man looked around them to the distance in all directions. "I wonder what happened to Sloan and his boys, they just leave or what?"

"Who cares," Took shot back. "He's always disappearing and then comes back to raise more hell with us – forget him."

Felts looked at each of the men. "You know what my question is? Where's Mel Johns right now? How come he didn't come to see Farley buried?"

"Forget him too; he's gone yella on us. He was just a lot of talk. Who's riding? I'm leaving now."

Each man tried to out-shout the others to prove his enthusiasm for the fight. Making their way back to the tied horses the men angrily jerked the reins loose and mounted. Kicking spurs to their horses, they headed for the Juniper at a gallop.

After a mile had disappeared under them the excitement had worn off and the men pulled their lathered horses down to a walk. The relieved horses dug deep for air, their sides heaving in exhaustion. The pace had slowed, but not the angry drive to get even with Brian Richards and his friends.

It was decided among them that as soon as they entered the ranch yard Felts and Took would storm the house, kick in the door, and shoot down Richards in his own parlor room. The other four men would spread out in pairs, going through the place as fast as they could shooting anyone they saw and setting everything on fire. They were determined to finish off the Englishman's reign in the high desert.

Reaching a rise above the ranch yard the men stopped and studied the house and surrounding sheds and barns. No men were in sight, but the ringing of iron on an anvil echoed from the blacksmith's shop to their right. The bunkhouse, cook shack, and corrals were deserted as all the men were off on the range.

With jaws set, the six men followed the plan and spread out through the place. Racing their horses up to the house, Took and Felts bounded out of their saddles and ran up the porch steps. With guns drawn Felts cocked back his leg and slammed his boot against the door, ripping the latch through the door jamb and exploding the pieces of wood into the room.

The first thing Earl Felts focused on was the two gaping black holes of the ten gauge shotgun held solidly in Henry Holden's hands. The blast blew him back out the door. Their attack was not as much of a surprise as they had thought. The time they wasted on the rise studying the place was enough for Henry to get set

Chic Took caught one of the stray lead pellets in his neck. Cursing in surprise and pain, the force of the shotgun blast and Felts' hurtling body knocked him to the floor boards of the porch; he somersaulted backwards and off the porch to the dirt below. He clapped a hand over the wound on his neck and looked up at the man calmly aiming the shotgun at him. He also saw that his gun was lying on the porch behind the man.

For a long moment the two men looked at each other. Then, stepping backwards, Henry toed Took's gun and kicked it at him. The heavy gun slid across the boards and landed on the prone man's chest.

Taking a step forward, Henry looked down on Took. "This bad business has come to an end; I will not shoot an unarmed man so there you have your gun – pick it up."

He had seen the Englishman in town when he so coolly wiped out Sloan's men. The Englishman had ice water in his veins and intended to shoot him one way or the other, whether he picked up the gun or not. He grabbed for the gun on his chest.

Kenny Weaver heard the second heavy blast as a man with a rifle ran into his shop. Holding the shaping hammer in his right hand and a metal bar glowing red hot in his left he shouted at the man. "What do you want?"

"I want every one of you dead."

Weaver grinned at him, "The devil you say."

The man lifted the rifle and made two quick steps forward. He didn't realize that he had closed the distance between the two of them just enough.

Kenny Weaver was a man who loved to fight. The grin widened as he thrust the glowing bar into the man's face. Instantly the man screamed out in pain as the stench and smoke of burning flesh filled his nostrils. Pulling the bar back Weaver swung it hard, the impact against the man's skull was solid. He was dead when he hit the ground, his hair smoldering where the bar had made its deadly connection with his head.

The sound of a shot filled the shop; Weaver felt the bullet hit him hard on the hip, spinning him to the ground. A second shot hit an inch from the first. He felt the burning pain and the blood soaking his pants under the leather apron. He looked up to see a tall whip of a man coming toward him pointing a revolver at his head.

Still holding the hammer in his right hand, Weaver planted his boot into the dirt and spun his big body in an arch. As he spun toward his attacker, he came down with all his strength driving the hammer down on the man's foot. With a howl of pain the gunman fell forward landing next to Weaver. The hammer fell again and two men lay dead in Kenny Weaver's blacksmith shop.

He could hear shots echoing throughout the ranch yard, but the bullets seemed to have broken his hip and he was unable to get up or out of the shop. Then he smelled smoke. Forcing his will against the pain, he dragged himself to the door way and looked out. The barn opposite him was on fire. Looking toward the house, he made out two bodies in the dirt below the porch. How many attackers there were was unknown. He could only lay on the ground and watch.

Bill Anthony had spread himself out between the two ranches. With Sam down he took it upon himself to oversee the operations on the original Juniper as well as his own responsibilities on Juniper East. Brian Richards had enough on his mind without worrying about cattle too, that was his job and he was taking care of business.

With the summer heading into August it was necessary to keep the cattle moving into new areas of the range. The grass was drying out and in order to prevent damage to the future graze, they were only allowed to stay put for a day or two. Bill and his crew were pushing a small herd to the eastern edge of the ranch when the pillar of thick smoke caught their attention.

The men stopped and stared, trying to mark the fire's location. Frank Perry stood in the stirrups and stretched his neck up for a better view. "Hey Bill, what do you make of that?"

"I don't know, but it's a hot fire."

Taking a calculation of the distance, Bill figured the smoke to be a good mile off and due east of them. "It's got to be on the ranch."

Frank sat back down in the saddle and anxiously looked at his friend. "The boss at home today?"

"No, he left this morning for Buchanan with Abby and Katy."

"Who's there then?"

Bill's expression matched Frank's, "Just Henry, and maybe Weaver."

"Then we'd better be riding – and fast."

Bill shouted back at the men to keep on with the cattle work. He and Frank then jumped their horses forward in a race across the sagebrush.

The remaining two attackers had no idea that their partners were all dead. They had encountered no one to slow them from setting fires. They were pleased with themselves that the barn was fully in flames and now a second shed was spreading flame and gray smoke.

They had heard the shooting and felt confident that Took and Felts had found the Englishman and killed him. They were flushed with the feeling of success, all there was left to do now was to finish burning the place down. Each man grabbed a burning board from the shed and headed for the chuck house. Running across the open area in front of the building they were stopped up short when the cook stepped out the door, raised a pistol and began shooting at them.

Both men dropped the burning boards and ran back for the cover of the burning shed. Determined to succeed they split up, each running to opposite sides of the chuck house and coming back together behind it.

One of the men laughed, "Let's fire it with that man inside and burn it down on top of him, if he runs we'll gun him down."

His partner joined the laugh and pulled a match out of his pocket. "Go grab a bunch of that dead brush over there and we'll light 'er up."

Keeping low to the ground the man reached the brush, yanked a dead plant out of the sand and returned to the building. Breaking the dry twigs into tinder they piled it under the weather-dried boards of the wall. The match was struck and laid on the tinder creating an instant burst of flame. They continued to feed the fuel to the flames until the fire was well up the side of the building.

When the fire was burning to their satisfaction they ran back to the cover of the sage and waited. Their wait was a short one before the cook came running out with a bucket of water. As he rounded the corner of the building the two men opened fire on him. Throwing the water at the fire, the cook spun on his heels and made his way back to the open door and jumped inside.

The water had managed to splash on the flames, but the growing heat was too much for it and little was done to slow the spread. The two men came to their feet and ran for a loafing shed and its surrounding corral. Laughing and shouting, they ignored all else that was going on around them until the two horsemen cut them off.

The laughter froze in their throats as the riders came down on them at a hard run. The first one raised his gun, but never got it level before Bill Anthony's .45 slug buried his third button into his ribs.

Frank Perry ran his horse over the second man sending him spinning wildly into a big sage plant. Reining hard around on his buckskin, Frank charged back at the dazed man. Pulling his rope off his saddle he deftly flipped open a loop, spun it once over his head and shot it out and over the man's head. Pulling the loop closed he dallied the rope off to the horn and yanked the man down on his head.

The buckskin was trained to keep a tight rope on whatever was at the end of it. He expertly stepped back each time the man tried to gain his feet, keeping the rope tight around his neck. Gasping for air with his face a dark red, the man finally stopped fighting and lay still on the ground.

Frank looked toward the chuck house, and saw that George just about had the fire out. Between buckets of water and shovelfuls of sand thrown against the building the flames were dying. The back wall was blackened and smoldering, but the damage had been minimal due to George's quick action.

Looking past the chuck house the shed was nothing but ashes and the barn beyond hope. He felt a surge of anger flare up inside him as he redirected his attention back to the man on the ground. Moving his horse toward him he watched as the man's eyes bugged out in fear and from the choking rope still around his neck.

Stopping within a hoof step of the man's head Frank looked down at him. "Bill, do you know what this is?"

Bill shook his head and then shrugged, "A pile of horse manure?"

"Yeah, pretty close. This here's Stinker Harlan, a shiftless no-account pile of horse manure if one ever lived. Stinker here would rather drink than work and figures it's everyone else's fault that he doesn't have anything. He doesn't like to take a bath either."

Bill spit a stream of tobacco juice that hit next to him and splashed up on his filthy shirt. "That right *Stinker*? You figure its Brian Richards' fault that you're a worthless lazy dog?"

Harlan pried his fingers between his neck and the tight noose that held him. Between gasps and choking he managed to squeak out the word, "Please."

Frank hissed, "Please? Please what? Please let me go? After you've burned half this ranch down? I think I should just throw this rope over a tree limb and finish the job. What do you think about that, Stinker?"

Frank backed the buckskin until the rope was tight again and the loop retightened back around Stinker's neck. The man's eyes went even wilder than they had been. He fought the rope in desperation, which only resulted in making the buckskin back up pulling the noose tighter and dragging him through the sand. Frank made no effort to stop the horse.

He pulled the horse to a stop and then moved him back toward Stinker. "I've got a better idea for you Stinker. We're going to send you back to town with that rope burn around your neck so you can show the rest of that outfit what's going to happen to them."

A movement caught both men's eye and they turned to see Henry walking toward them carrying the shotgun. Bill shouted out, "How many were there Henry?"

"Six, counting him and that one." He pointed at the man Bill had shot.

"Six! Where's the others?"

"Two tried to break into the house and never made it. Two more tried to kill Kenny; you do not want to see what is left of them."

"You, George, and Kenny the only ones here?"

"Yes, and Kenny is wounded and in need of the doctor."

Frank motioned for Bill to pull the rope off of Stinker. Bill roughly yanked the hemp rope off the man's neck causing him to yell out in pain as it sawed into the already raw and bleeding flesh. Stinker was crying as he tried to stand on his shaking legs, fell, and then managed to stand.

"You have a horse Stinker?"

The man nodded and then fell back down in a sitting position.

"You get on him and head back for town. Like I said, you show everyone your neck and tell them about your dead friends. You might have to draw them pictures because I doubt that your voice is going to be working too good for a while, but you make sure and get the point across."

Both men moved their horses away from Stinker, who was shakily struggling to his feet. The fear had made his legs too weak to hold him and he fell several times before he finally was able to make it across the distance to where the horses had been left.

"Let's get Kenny in the wagon and get him to town. I guess he'll be in next to Sam for a while."

Reaching the blacksmith shop, they found Weaver lying on his left side with his heavy apron off. He was holding a handful of rags against his hip.

Frank shook his head, "Kenny, you're bound to get poisoning from them dirty rags."

"I'm okay." The big man growled.

Frank chuckled. "Did the bullets go in or did they bounce off that bull hide of yours?"

"I got two holes and I think a broke hip, I guess they went in."

"Then, I'd say you're *not* okay. We're taking you to the Doc."

Weaver nodded his approval. "I guess so; at least I'm not as bad off as Sam."

Dismounting the two men looked around the shop. Bill grimaced, "I see what Henry meant about them two boys there."

Frank shook his head, "Their own mothers wouldn't know them, providing they ever even had mothers."

The rattle of the buckboard came to them as Henry pulled it around the shop. With Weaver helping the best he could, it still took all of them to get him in the wagon. Frank wiped his brow, "I swear, Weaver, I've lifted smaller cattle."

Stepping back away from the wagon Bill motioned to Frank, "You and Henry take him on in; I'll see what I can do here. I want to be here when Mister Richards gets home."

Bill watched the wagon rock its way along the road until it was out of sight. He stood in the middle of the battlefield and looked around him. The silence after the din of gunshots and loud voices was eerie. The wind blew its way through the junipers whipping the smoke off the last standing boards of the barn's frame, and stirred the ashes and glowing embers that had only an hour before been a barn and a shed. He shook his head in disbelief that such carnage was brought on them by their so-called neighbors, it was unbelievable.

He knew there was no going back now, the fight was on. The man he knew Brian Richards to be would not stand by wringing his hands in fear wondering what to do next. This thing could only end with the death of Harper Sloan or Brian Richards, and his money was on Richards. What was it Devon had said? Down to the last man? The crashing of the charcoaled barn framing emphasized the thought. It was all about to come crashing down alright, right down on the heads of the Juniper's enemies.

Chapter 14

The rush of the stream cascading down the canyon, twisting around boulders like snipe on the wing and slinging spray into the low boughs of the firs, would normally have held Devon's attention. It was like a painting and he had always loved the beauty of nature, but this morning it was lost to him as he watched Norm Dinton.

Dinton stood on a high bank looking down into the stream. In his right hand he held a tin cup of coffee, in his left a rock. Sipping at the coffee, he watched the white water for several minutes then tossed the rock into the swirl of white. He smiled as if he had accomplished something and turned back to his waiting prisoners sitting beside the fire.

He jabbed his thumb over his shoulder, "There's been a mint of gold taken out of that stream. In fact this whole area is booming with gold, some folks are making a sight of money these days."

Devon and Trig merely looked at him with no comment while Sloan and Jackson went on saddling their horses and ignoring him.

"Yep, some men are coming in here with rags on their backs and ending up in San Francisco suits." Then puffing out his chest he added, "Baker City's the up and coming place around these parts. Virginia City's playing out and we're the big place now. A man in my position could make out pretty good. I might be wearing one of those San Francisco suits myself one of these days."

Devon and Trig exchanged glances and noticed that Sloan was giving his partner the same look. It was apparent that Marshal Dinton was not a liked man, but one to be used. Leading his horse back to the fire Sloan looked at Dinton and then down to the two men sitting by the fire.

"I think we need to get these two up and have them saddling some horses so we can get on with this. I have business to attend to and don't have any time to be wasting on your history lessons."

Dinton frowned and tossed the last of his coffee into the fire. "If I recall properly, Mister Sloan, I'm doing you a favor, not the other way around."

"Maybe, but you're going to come out looking pretty good on this. Arresting two big time cattle rustlers is going to put a feather in your cap with your boss. The longer we sit here the longer before you get that feather."

Neither Devon nor Trig moved as Dinton poured the remains of the pot on the fire and kicked dirt over it. "Get up and saddle your horses, we'll be in town by noon."

Devon gave him a cold look, "I see who's running this show."

Dinton shot him a hate-filled glare. "That's right McCloud, I'm running this show."

Devon looked from Dinton to Sloan and chuckled, "Sure you are."

Trig turned his attention to Sloan. "You know Sloan, I've just been wracking my brain trying to figure out what your part is in all this. I know you well enough to know that you don't do anything unless there's something in it for you, and I can't see you giving a hoot about the likes of Charlie Sampson, so what is it?"

Sloan grinned, "Parker, you always were one to do too much thinking. Thinking can get a man killed."

Trig matched the grin. "Or keep him from it."

"I have my reasons."

Rolling his eyes back Trig groaned. "Not the speech about saving the country from the English. That story's about as lame as a four dollar horse."

A burst of laughter broke from Sloan. "Those square-heads in Drewsey believe it, why don't you?"

"Because my head ain't square."

"Well, stop wracking your brain, you won't figure it out. Besides, you're going to be in a jail cell and can't do anything about it anyway. By the time you get out, it'll be all over."

Devon broke in, "So that's the purpose behind all this? You get this poor excuse for a lawman to arrest us on false charges and get us a long ways out of the way while you try to wipe out Brian Richards. Am I close?"

Sloan smirked, "You're being arrested for cattle theft and that's the whole thing. You can make up all the tales you want, but mister you're on your way to jail for stealing Chuck Sampson's cattle."

"It won't matter if we're there or not. Brian has enough good men to put a stop to whatever your plan is."

"Maybe, but we've got a lot of men too. Richards is finished and what he did to Charlie will catch up to him."

Devon matched the outlaw's smirk, "Now who's telling tales?"

"That's enough of this nonsense," Dinton stood over Devon. "You boys get saddled; we're heading out – now."

Trig motioned for Devon to go to the horses while he made like he was getting up. When the attention was off of him Trig took a chunk of charred wood from the fire and quickly scrawled 'bakr' on a rock and then got to his feet and followed Devon.

Devon looked back at Trig and asked the question with his eyes.

"I left something for Hack to find."

"Think he can track us this far?"

"Five horses leave plenty of sign, he'll figure it out."

Dinton turned around and eyed them suspiciously; he cast a look around and behind them trying to figure out what they were talking about. Seeing nothing out of the ordinary he faced forward, flipped the off-side rein around his horse's neck and stepped into the saddle. Reining the horse halfway around, he watched silently as his two prisoners bridled and saddled their horses. His attention went from them back to Sloan and Jackson, who were growing tired of the wait.

Sloan's paper-thin patience finally snapped, "You two going to take all day to saddle them horses or are you just trying to waste time?"

Devon's eyes flickered in annoyance, his own patience was wearing thin and Sloan was grinding his heels on the last of it. Trig grinned and then laughed.

The laugh cut into the outlaw. "You're a smart one Parker, but you're not holding any of the cards here. If I was you I'd be a whole lot more careful how I talked."

"Talked? I never said a word."

"You didn't have to."

Trig pulled the cinch on his horse and turned around to face Sloan. "I'm not wearing a gun Sloan, now's the best chance you'll ever get to kill me. The day'll come when I will be, and I'll be looking for you, so you'd best do it now."

Sloan glared down at Trig, the debate raging in his mind. He wanted to do it, to kill this man he secretly feared, but Trig had friends and he knew there would be no end to it if he did."

Trig pointed toward Dinton, "Of course you'd have to kill the Marshal too."

Sloan's face soured, "It wouldn't be the first time."

Devon pulled the stirrup off his saddlehorn and let it drop. Turning he looked squarely at Dinton, who was looking sick and squirming in his saddle. "Is that what happened to Willard Vaughn?"

Dinton stared back in silence. The color was draining from his face and his eyes were showing fear. Slowly he shook his head, "I don't know what happened to Willard."

Tipping his head toward Sloan Devon stated flatly, "He does, ask him."

"No one knows what happened to him. He was headed for John Day and just never came back. We all just figure he's dead, either thrown from his horse or shot by some crazy miner."

Devon looked at the outlaw, "Is that right Sloan?"

Sloan shrugged his shoulders, "No business of mine, I never cared for the man and, to tell you the truth, I don't care what happened to him."

Devon gave each man a long look and then nodded his head. Turning back around he toed the stirrup and swung his leg over the horse's back. "We'd better get moving so you can lock us up and get us out of the way."

Touching spurs to his horse Sloan rode up beside Devon, "You might not ever get out of that cell. A lot of things can happen to a cattle thief in these parts." Then he chuckled, "You two boys might get real friendly with a short length of hemp."

With a casual turn of his head Devon looked at Sloan, "Don't get too comfortable, that length of hemp might end up with *your* name on it."

"You talk too much McCloud." With that he pulled his horse back and dropped in behind the two prisoners.

The rest of the morning passed slowly as all talk ended with Devon's questions about Marshal Vaughn and his *hemp* prediction for Sloan. He had hit a nerve in Dinton and Sloan both. It was clear to him that both men were part of Vaughn's killing; to what extent was the question that remained, but from the fear he saw in

Dinton's eyes the man knew more than he was letting on.

The closer they drew to the city the more travelers they met on the road. Men in wagons, on horseback, and an occasional family indicated that this was a regular route in and out of town. He was surprised that Dinton had chosen such a route to bring them in on, but then again maybe he was showing off.

Trig leaned over toward him, "Watch the men we pass, look at their faces when they come up to Dinton."

Devon began to pay attention to the men they passed and he soon picked up on what Trig meant. There were no greetings exchanged with the Marshal, only scowls and looks of disgust. The same look was held as they looked over Sloan and Jackson. That the three men were known by the locals was evident, it was also as evident that they were not well thought of.

"I see what you mean." Devon watched a pair of riders come toward them and pass. "I'd say that if there was a hanging for our friends here every man in this town would be pulling on the rope."

Trig nodded, "That's exactly what I mean."

Devon grinned, "Which would explain why they didn't kill us. They already have enough folks looking at them without two known ranchers turning up dead after having a run-in with Dinton and his friends."

"That does give us an edge," Trig grinned back at Devon. "That *does* give us an edge."

Coming into the business district of town, Devon began to notice the large number of mining related businesses lining the streets. Mining companies, assayers, and signs mounted on all the buildings inviting those with gold to come in and spend it. Suddenly the face of Jonah Welsh loomed up in his mind. He wondered if his old partner had found his mother lode and stayed around or moved on. It could prove to be helpful if he was still here.

Dinton turned his horse off the street and into a side alley that turned out to be the side entrance to the Marshal's Office. "Here we are boys, your new home for awhile."

Trig gave Dinton a sarcastic smirk, "This the jail, or the graveyard?"

Having arrived safely to his home ground Dinton's confidence was again growing. "It's up to you; it could be either one you want it to be."

Lifting his chin toward Sloan and Jackson Trig added, "Will we have a cell next to them two?"

Dinton gave a mock expression of surprise. "What? My two trusted Deputies?"

"Not us," Sloan broke in. "We've got to get back to Drewsey, unfinished business and all – you know how that is."

Dinton stepped off his horse and pulled his gun. Pointing it at Devon and Trig, he puffed out his chest. "Now get off them horses and get inside."

Looking around Devon saw no one watching them. "Put up the gun Dinton, no one's watching so you're wasting your show."

Dinton's face flushed red. Pushing the door open he growled, "Get in."

Devon and Trig stepped inside the office while Dinton brushed past them, snatched a ring of keys off a nail in the wall, and moved toward a closed wooden door with a window in the upper half. Opening it, he gestured with his still drawn gun for them to go through it. They went in with Sloan and Jackson blocking their back.

"Go in that open cell right there."

Both men walked into the cell and heard the loud clang of the iron door swinging shut behind them. Dinton shoved the key in the lock and turned it with a resolute snap. Turning, he walked back out of the cell area and closed the wooden door leaving the two men alone in the jail.

Walking to the back of the cell, Devon looked up at a barred window above his head that wasn't more than a foot-and-a-half square. Standing on the bunk he could look out between the bars to the alley they had entered from. He couldn't see them, but he heard two horsemen ride out of the alley.

"I think Sloan and Jackson just headed out."

Stepping back off the bunk he sat down and began to think. "When I first came to Drewsey I had a partner with me name of Jonah Welsh. When we parted ways he was heading for Baker City to get rich on gold. I need to find out if he's still here; if he is he might be able to help us."

"Well, there's one way to find out." Digging into his hip pocket Trig pulled out two silver dollars. Holding them up between his thumb and fingers he grinned. Stepping up on the bunk he pressed his face against the bars and waited. His vision was limited to what was directly in front of him, but he could listen.

After a few minutes he heard the sound of running feet growing closer to the window. A boy ran across his line of vision, before the boy could pass Trig called out to him in a low voice. "Kid, hey kid, stop."

The boy dug his feet into the dirt and slid to a stop. He looked up at the barred window more from curiosity than obedience. "What?"

Holding the dollars in front of his face Trig went on. "You want to make a couple of dollars?"

The boy was about ten years old, and with men earning a dollar a day in wages, two dollars was a fortune. "Sure."

"You know a man named Jonah Welsh? He's a gold miner."

The boy looked at him like he was addled, "Everyone's a gold miner around here."

Trig tossed a dollar out to the boy who deftly caught it in mid-air. "You find Jonah Welsh and tell him Devon McCloud's in Marshal Dinton's jail. You do that and I'll give you the other dollar."

The boy buried the big coin in his pocket. "Marshal Dinton put you in there?"

"He sure did."

My Pa says Marshal Dinton is a four-flusher and a tinhorn. Pa says Marshal Vaughn was a good man and Dinton killed him."

"Your Pa knows Dinton pretty good. Now go."

As the boy's footfalls faded away Trig came down off the bunk and sat down on it. "Well, now we wait."

Devon grinned at him, "You seem sort of at home in here."

"I've been in jail a time or two, but I never done it."

"Never done what?"

Trig grinned, "Whatever it was they put me in jail for."

Hack Parker leaned to the side and studied the ground from his saddle. He had found the first camp and had been following the horseshoe prints ever since. He was wandering farther east and north then he had ever been before. He had no idea where the men who had his brother and Devon were going, but he intended to stay on them until he found out.

The trail began to climb up into the timber, winding its way between the tall firs and pines. They were moving like men who had a destination; they weren't wandering like riders with no purpose in mind. The fact that he had not come across their bodies and five horses were still on the trail was a good sign. There was obviously no intention of killing the two men, they were being taken somewhere for whatever reason, which meant they could eventually be found.

Afternoon found him working his way up a steep canyon with a fast moving stream racing along the canyon's bottom. Coming out on a wide flat area he immediately spotted the remains of a camp fire. Looking around he found where the horses had been tied. The prints pounded into the ground where the horses had stood for hours were the same ones he had been following since Abby and Katy found the guns on the ranch road. Going back to the black remains of the fire he studied it for a moment and found nothing that would help him. He began to turn away when some letters on a flat rock caught his eye.

Picking up the rock he strained to make out the figures. He and Trig had been spending time with Abby learning their letters and how to read. He was coming along with it, but still had a ways to go. "B-A-K-R", he spoke the letters out loud.

Struggling to put the word together he remembered Abby's lessons on sounding out vowels and letters. Struggling to make out the word, it suddenly burst into his mind. "Baker!" he shouted out loud. "Baker City, that's where they're going."

Tossing the rock into the stream he swung onto his horse and put him back on the trail. He was proud of himself for having solved the word, he knew now, more than ever, how important learning to read was. He vowed to become as good as Aunt Abby at it, but right now he needed to find his brother. He had no idea where Baker City was, but he knew he could find it.

Chapter 15

The smoke from the dying fires was down to ghost-like wisps tossed on the breeze when the wagon rolled slowly into the yard. Brian Richards surveyed the damage in stunned silence as he rode ahead of it. Bill Anthony came off the house's porch and walked toward him.

Richards' expression was weary, but his eyes burned with anger as he looked down at his ranch manager. "What happened Bill?"

"Our so-called neighbors *'happened'*, Mister Richards. I was off at the main ranch when they hit. It was only Henry, George, and Kenny here."

"How many were there?"

"Six. Henry shotgunned two of them at the house and Kenny killed two in the blacksmith's shop. Frank and I got here just in time to stop the last two from firing the chuck house and killing George. We killed one of them and sent the last one back with a burned neck and a message."

Richards looked at him curiously, "Burned neck?"

"Frank roped him and dragged him around a bit."

Richards nodded his understanding. "Any of our people hurt?"

"Kenny got shot, but he'll be alright. Frank and Henry took him into town."

"Was Harper Sloan with them?"

"No, just some of the local idiots."

Abby held her place on the wagon seat and looked around. "It could have been a lot worse Brian."

Turning his head he looked at her, "Yes, it could have been much worse."

"They could have burned your house and killed all your men; as it is you lost a barn, a shed, and had one man winged."

Richards moved his horse toward the chuck house. "There is always something to be thankful for I guess."

Bill tipped his hat toward the women. "Reckon I'll wander around and keep a watch out for any more trouble."

Marie sat in shock. Despite the warm air of the oncoming evening, she felt chills run through her. Abby had explained the situation to her, but she was not prepared to witness the actual results of the fight.

Abby recognized the shocked look. "Are you all right, Marie?"

"Yes, but this is so terrible."

"It is that and until we can put an end to Harper Sloan it's going to keep bein' terrible."

"Why are they doing this? We never had such problems in Kansas; everyone respected each other's property."

"That's what we can't figure out. We all respect each other's property here too and that's why this is so bad. It's still all a mystery on why they want to run Brian out so bad."

Marie turned her head slightly and watched Brian ride away from them. "I can't imagine what he could have ever done to warrant such abuse; he seems like a nice man."

Abby smiled slightly, "Even if he is English?"

Marie's head snapped around to face Abby. She was silent for a second, "Was I that obvious?"

"You did look pretty surprised when he first opened his mouth and that English accent came out."

"Yes, I'm afraid Mister Richards did notice, didn't he?"

Abby nodded, "That's why he said what he did Marie, he's a good friend and I think he'd like to be your friend too."

"Seeing all this and thinking back on my behavior I feel so bad. I am ashamed."

Abby waved her hand in front of her, "Don't be, folks come out here with all sorts of ideas and behaviors that they were raised with. We all learn to live together and accept each other for what we are. Out here we judge folks by their courage, honor, and work, not by appearances or family. That's what makes this so terrible; it was done by folks who should be Brian's neighbors, but they're judging him as being a foreigner who needs to be run out."

"I can see why Devon took on his fight. He was raised to be concerned about others and fight for just causes. English or not, this is wrong."

"Yes, it is, and you can be right proud of your son, there's no back-up in him."

"Just like his father. He was a man quick to fight when the need arose."

Abby put her hand on Marie's shoulder, "We've been through this once and we came out ahead – we will again."

George came out of the chuck house wiping his hands on his flour sack apron. He took a few steps out to meet Richards and stopped.

"Are you all right, George?"

"Yes sir, I am. I'm not sure if I would be though, if Bill and Frank hadn't shown up when they did. Those yahoos had the place on fire, but I got it out before it did any real damage."

Richards forced a small smile, "You are an enduring man George."

"It's nothing."

"This is quite different from Sacramento. I am sure you had no idea you would be dodging bullets when you came here."

George waved the statement off with a flip of his wrist. "I was working in that hotel in Sacramento because I got stuck there without any money, and then I stayed because of the money; I'm really a man of the West. I've cooked more trail drive meals and fed more cowpunchers than I ever did folks in a fancy hotel, and I've seen more than one fight, and been in a few myself. This is no big deal Mister Richards, it's where I belong."

"I never knew that George, I am impressed."

"Now, I have some supper ready so bring your friends on in. Come on now, before it all turns to slop."

Richards felt his spirits lift a bit; George's casual attitude about the whole affair seemed infectious. It was hard to stay upset when the people around you refused to give into a feeling of being beaten. He began to realize that Abby was right it could have been a lot worse. Reining his horse around he rode back to the wagon and the waiting women.

"Ladies, George has supper ready, go in and eat. You too Abby, I will see to your team."

Abby whispered behind her to Katy, "Take Marie on in, I want to talk to Brian."

Watching from her seat, Abby waited for Katy and Marie to walk out of hearing range. Motioning with her head toward a corral

Abby spoke low to Richards, "I'll go with you."

Realizing that she wanted to talk, Richards followed the wagon until Abby pulled the horses to a stop at the corral gate. Dismounting, he began to unbuckle the harness. Abby put her hand on his arm; he stopped his work and looked at her.

"Brian, I know how you feel right now, but not everyone around here is like that bunch. There's some mighty good folks in these parts, but most tend to just mind their own business. You do have friends in town and you have us and you know that we'll fight with you right down to the wire."

"I know, but thank you for saying it. I appreciate the support. Sometimes just a reminder that one has friends at a time like this is enough to see you through the troubles."

"You have the best crew around for three states; your men are loyal to you."

"I know that as well, but look at Sam, lying on his deathbed because of his loyalty to me." A dark shadow of doubt crossed Richards' face.

"You were a soldier weren't you?"

"Yes."

"Did you fight for the Queen and for country, ready to lay your life down out of honor and loyalty?"

Surprised by the question Richards shifted his feet and stood a bit straighter. "Of course."

"Then would you expect less from a man like Sam Raven?"

He had not considered the situation in those terms. Turning his eyes to the ground he pondered the comparison, and then looked back up. "I never thought of it in that way, Sam is doing for me and the Juniper exactly what I would do."

The corners of Abby's mouth turned up and her voice took on a tone of cheer. "There you have it, your men are warriors, and you *will* win this fight."

The shadow disappeared from Richards' face. "Yes, we will win this fight. With good friends and loyal men, we will indeed win."

A look of mischief suddenly filled Abby's eyes as she looked up at her friend. "Speaking of friends, I think a certain widow would like to be better friends with a proper British gentleman that I know."

Richard's expression went blank. "Who?"

Abby gave him an annoyed look. "How many widows have you met lately?"

"Marie, I mean Mrs. McCloud? That's nonsense; I frightened the poor woman half to death with my speech."

"At first, but not now."

"I understand her raising and the horrors her ancestors endured from my people; she has no love for the English."

"People change Brian. Devon did. Give her a chance, she feels pretty bad about her reaction to you and I think she would like to make amends. Talk to her at supper and see for yourself."

Shaking his head Richards argued, "It is improper, she has only been widowed less than a year."

"In these parts that don't matter, we don't hold to any particular custom on such things. A woman alone out here can have a frightening future facing her. Besides, I never said that you should run right out and marry her, just be her friend and let it go from there."

"If that is the case, then why did you not remarry?"

Abby shrugged, "Didn't want to, didn't need to, and I had Katy."

"Mrs. McCloud has Devon and you."

"She just met us and we are all becoming friends at the same time, you might as well too. We don't know what will happen to Devon either; she will need friends one way or the other."

The shadow returned to Richard's face. "Yes, Devon, I trust his abilities and fighting strength, but I fear for him as well."

"Me too. All the more reason for Marie to feel secure and safe here."

Richards gave in to her argument, "Yes, I see. I will try and be her friend."

Abby patted him on the arm. "Good, now let's finish unhitching this team and go get some supper."

The last of the daylight was fading into darkness as the two friends walked quietly toward the chuckhouse. The smell of smoke hung heavy in the air and the last glowing embers of the fires sparkled in the darkness. All served as reminders that the fight was not finished and more blood was bound to be spilled before it was.

Opening the door, the light of the room flooded out into the night. Taking two lanterns down from their pegs on the outside wall Richards turned around and hung them from nails on the building's porch poles. Lifting the glass on the first one, he lit the wick and lowered the glass, he repeated the process for the second one. The lanterns formed a circle of glaring light.

He turned back to see Abby watching him. "I want to be sure Henry and Frank can find their way in."

Together they went inside and closed the door. Katy sat silently with a full plate in front of her. Biting her bottom lip she looked up at her mother.

Abby put her arm around her. "Eat, you need your strength."

"I can't, first Devon and now this. It's too much like last year ... even worse."

Marie sat on the bench seat across the long table from the two. She looked first at Abby with worry and then to Katy with the eyes of a concerned mother. Reaching her hand across the table she took Katy's hand. "Don't worry dear, Devon will come back to you safe and sound."

Katy nodded, but tears began to roll down her cheeks.

Abby sat down next to her. "Enough of that, you need to be strong right now. Devon needs to know that you're here for him and we all need to be ready to fight back."

Wiping her cheeks Katy nodded again. "I know – I will be."

"Now eat, you've got someone else depending on you to eat for them."

Marie's face lit up as she looked at Abby, her eyes asking the silent question. Abby nodded and smiled. Returning her attention to Katy, she smiled at her. "When?"

Katy sniffed and smiled back. "The doctor said sometime just after the first of the year."

"Oh, how wonderful!"

Katy's dark mood began to lift as the attention of the two women regarding their grandchild cheered her.

With a cup of coffee in hand Richards made his way around the table and sat down next to Marie. He only smiled as he listened to the women talking excitedly about the baby and the bright prospects for the future. He was happy to see that the problems of the moment were put behind the bright prospects of tomorrow.

George came out of his kitchen carrying a platter of meat in one hand and a bowl of potatoes in the other. Setting them on the table he looked at Katy's untouched meal and shook his head. "Katy, if you don't eat that meal I'm likely to think you don't like my cooking."

"Sorry George, I'll eat it, I promise."

"You'd better. Besides if that youngster starts eating my grub now he won't be a stranger to it when he comes around later to visit this old man."

Katy laughed, "What if it's a *she*?"

"Then I'll put a pink napkin on the table, now eat."

The sound of a wagon coming toward the building caught everyone's attention. Brian got up and walked toward the door, George followed him. Opening the door, Richards stepped out and waited. The wagon soon came into the lantern light revealing Frank and Henry sitting on the seat. As they were pulling the horses to a stop, he could see the big frame of Kenny Weaver in the back.

"I'm happy to see you men have returned safely. How is Kenny?"

The deep rough voice coming from the dark made Richards smile. "I'm fine boss."

Bill came running up as the men were climbing down. He gave Frank a hand helping Weaver out of the wagon.

Richards watched as the big man came down from the wagon bed, sliding two crutches under his arms he hobbled his way to the lighted doorway. "Doc says I have to use these for a few days until the hip starts to heal, at least it ain't broke."

The men filed in the door. "Oh boy," Frank sighed, "Food, I'm about starved to death."

The men did not see the women until they were fully in the room, as one they removed their hats and greeted them. They then sat down at the table that was set up in front of the one the women sat at.

Weaver was grumbling his frustration as he tried to manipulate the clumsy crutches around the table. Finally he was able to get himself to where he could slide in on the end of the bench seat. Letting out a long exhausted breath he turned his head toward Richards. "This ain't nothing boss; I'll be up and pounding iron tomorrow morning."

"You will do no such thing."

Weaver looked at him with surprise. "I won't be working tomorrow?"

"No, you will be resting and healing that wound."

"Can't do that boss. Man don't work, he don't eat or get paid."

Richards frowned at Weaver. "On this ranch my men get fed and paid."

"Not if he can't work. A man who can't hold up his own ain't of no value to them around him."

"Mister Weaver, who owns this ranch?"

Weaver eyed him suspiciously as if the question was meant to trick him. "You do."

"Then who decides what happens to the men who work this ranch?"

"You do."

"Now that we have established who is in charge, I will begin again. Any man who becomes injured working for me will neither go unfed nor unpaid while he is recovering. End of argument Mister Weaver. Besides, you are the best blacksmith I have seen in years; I want you back on the job. If you don't rest you will not heal and if you don't eat you will waste away to skin and bones. I do not need a weak and skinny blacksmith. Am I clear?"

Weaver stared at Richards with his mouth hanging open. Closing his mouth he nodded his head. "Yes sir, I understand."

"Good." Richards then resumed his seat at the table next to Marie.

Marie looked at him, her expression revealing her approval of his actions. He caught her out of the corner of his eye, turned and smiled at her.

"That was very generous of you Mister Richards. Most employers would fire a man who couldn't work."

"Kenny was shot defending this ranch, only the smallest and weakest of men would not reward such loyalty. It is the least I can do for him."

"Mister Richards, I am impressed by such nobility and honor."

"Please Mrs. McCloud, call me Brian. We are neighbors and needn't be so formal."

Marie smiled, "Very well Brian, but then I insist you call me Marie."

Bowing his head toward her he smiled, "Marie it is then."

He glanced across the table and saw Abby's face and the mischief dancing in her eyes. He smiled back at her.

Chapter 16

The wounds in his back were burning and itching, the doctor had said they would and from his past experiences with wounds, they always did. It was uncomfortable, but a good indication that they were healing. He swung his legs out of the bed and planted his bare feet on the wood floor. It was a nice house, out of town and out of sight of eyes that didn't need to know anything just yet.

Slowly he got to his feet and walked to the wash basin on the table. He was happy to feel his old strength returning, he felt ready to take care of some unfinished business. Looking in the mirror he rubbed the rough growth on his jaws, he decided that the moustache was fine except for a few long hairs that needed to be trimmed to look neater, but he needed a shave. Flipping open his razor he laid it next to the basin and poured some water into it.

His face had lost some of its color, but the steel-blue eyes peering back at him had lost none of their fire. He was a man wronged and he intended to right it, such a thing makes a man recover from his wounds much quicker than one who would rather lay around and be nursed. He wasn't one to do that and the quicker he was back on the job, the better.

He shaved and then sat back down on the bed and pulled his socks and boots on. He was already feeling like his old self again, clean, shaven, and having his boots on he was ready to ride. Making his way down the stairs, he slid his hand along the polished hardwood handrail. It was indeed a nice house, the kind of house that he might like to have, but well out of his price range. Then again, he preferred the smell of a sage fire on the range or to hear the wind in the pines up high in the Blues. Baker City was filled with such houses, but not for him.

The woman who kept the house clean and cooked the meals met him at the entrance to the kitchen. Putting her hands on her hips she glared at him. "What are you doing out of bed? Doctor Putnam specifically told you to rest."

He looked at the woman and smiled, "I did rest Mrs. Young. A man can't stay to bed forever."

Mrs. Young pretended to be angry, like a mother hen, but the humor danced in her brown eyes. "Alright then, come in and have some breakfast, you can't heal unless you eat."

He sat down at the table and watched the woman fill a plate with enough food to feed two men. She was a tough one and he appreciated that, her gray hair hid none of the strength of character that was in her. He recalled the mine explosion that killed a half dozen miners, her husband among them. Soon after that she was hired to tend the house.

As he sat over his meal he considered the owner of the house, he was a good man; he knew a woman widowed had a rough row to hoe. He had been fortunate and shared that good fortune with others. It was only by the slightest of chances that this man had decided to travel to John Day that afternoon and found him lying face down bleeding to death in the road. Like the Good Samaritan in the Bible, he had packed him home and got a doctor to the house. He was also wise enough to realize that someone had tried to murder him and might try again, so he kept his presence at the house a secret. The doctor was a friend and had no problems with keeping the secret.

He heard the heavy wooden door open and then close again followed by boots on the hardwood floor. "Mrs. Young, I'm hungry as a bear, I sure hope you have some good breakfast for me."

Looking up from the stove she called back, "Mister Welsh, do you think I'd let you go hungry? Oh, and you have company for breakfast."

Jonah Welsh stepped briskly into the kitchen and laughed. "Willard, by the Lord, it's good to see you up and on the move."

"Thanks to you I am."

Jonah laughed, "Naw, you're a good man Willard, and this country needs good lawmen."

"Well, I appreciate that Jonah. What's the news out there since I've been out of commission?"

"There's been no word of Harper Sloan and his gang; they must have left the country after shooting you. Norm Dinton's filling in for you."

Willard Vaughn's face soured, "Norm Dinton, that bas...," he glanced up at Mrs. Young and caught himself before he said it. "I know he had a hand in this. He's rotten to the core, I know he's been taking bribes and I'd bet a silver dollar to a burned biscuit that he had a hand in setting me up to be killed."

Jonah looked at him, "I never liked the man, but do you think he'd go that far?"

"Oh yeah, he wants to be top dog around here and in order to do that he needs me out of the way. Besides, how else would Sloan have known where to find me? Only Dinton knew where I was going that day."

"That does add up alright. What are you going to do now?"

"Does he think I'm dead?"

"Everyone does. Not a soul except us and Doc Putnum knows you're here."

"Good, then it should come as a complete surprise to the weasel when I show back up."

"When do you figure on doing that?"

"Today."

"Today! You aren't up to that yet."

"Oh, I'm ready, I'm more than ready."

The discussion was cut short by a loud knocking at the door. Jonah got up and went out of the kitchen. Turning the knob, he opened the door to find a boy standing on the porch. Jonah smiled at him, "Can I help you son?"

"Mister Welsh, I have a message for you."

"Okay, let's have it."

"I was told to tell you that Marshal Dinton has Devon McCloud in his jail, and he needs your help."

Jonah's face fell. "Devon McCloud? Are you sure it was Devon McCloud?"

"Yes sir, that's what he said."

Digging into his pocket, Jonah pulled out a couple of coins and handed them to the boy. "Thanks son. Go back and tell Devon McCloud that I got the message."

Closing the door Jonah walked slowly back to the kitchen, his mind running back thinking about his old friend. As he entered the kitchen Vaughn looked up at him, "What happened Jonah? You look like you've seen a ghost."

"Sort of, I just got a message that an old friend of mine has been put in jail by Norm Dinton and he needs my help."

"Who is it?"

"Man name of Devon McCloud, we used to be partners."

Vaughn straightened in his seat, "Devon McCloud! I know Devon."

A look of surprise covered Jonah's face. "You know Devon?"

"Sure do. He was a big part of that fight over in the Strawberrys."

"I heard about that, a land grab or something wasn't it? Talk has it tagged as the Bitter Grass War."

"Yeah, that's what they're calling it. A couple of big money men tried to take a ranch away from a widow and her daughter. They would have too, if not for McCloud and a couple others. He fought for them and it was one heck of a fight. I ended up arresting the big cattleman involved and bringing him up here. He's in prison right now. In fact, I think that's why Sloan came after me, to avenge his brother. I couldn't swear to it, but I believe that was the reason. "

Jonah sat down across the table from Vaughn. "The Bitter Grass War. Devon had a hand in that?"

"Yep, he's quite a hand with a gun. Good thing he's a law abiding man or he'd be a lawman's nightmare."

"You ain't a-woofin', I've seen him use it. We parted ways up there just over a year ago, I came here and obviously he stayed."

Jonah sat silent for a minute. "You said Dinton was in with Harper Sloan and Sloan came after you because of what happened up there. Do you think Devon's being in jail right now has something to do with all that?"

"Could be. There were some bad characters involved in that whole affair. After what I learned at the trial I wasn't really surprised to see Sloan pop up, although I have to admit I didn't expect to be bushwhacked by his whole gang."

"What was it you learned at the trial?"

"Well, it turns out that Charles Sampson, the cattleman who tried to kill the widow and all, is really Charlie Sloan, Harper's brother."

"I know that name, Sampson." Jonah stared at the table top trying to recall why he knew the name. Jerking his head up he almost shouted, "Now I remember, Devon had a run-in with him in Drewsey over a mustang mare. So, he's one of the Sloans, was he hiding out or something?"

"Don't know the particulars of it, but at one time he ran with Harper and Travis Jackson. Jackson's their cousin."

"Willard, I know Devon, he's as honest as the day is long. If he's in jail it's not because of anything he did."

Vaughn stood up and pushed his chair back. "No, not McCloud. Let's go get him out of there."

Jonah gave him a doubtful look. "I still don't think you're up to this yet."

"Jonah, I can't thank you enough for what you did for me, but it's time to take my place back. I want to take Norm Dinton apart piece by piece, and get an innocent man out of jail. It's also time to put this whole Sloan business to an end once and for all. If I get half a chance I'll kill Harper Sloan and Jackson on sight."

Jonah turned and disappeared out of the kitchen for several minutes and then returned carrying two gun and holster sets. Handing one to Vaughn he grinned, "Here's your gun, let's go take care of business."

Jonah Welsh's house was only a mile from the edge of town; however it was back in the timber. Jonah liked his privacy and few people came to the house. It was a half-hour ride to the Marshal's Office where Norm Dinton held his prisoners. If he had been an honest lawman and had set out to solve Willard Vaughn's disappearance, he could have easily found him recuperating in a house just down the road, but he was content to believe his nemesis was dead.

Dinton was sitting behind the Marshal's desk with his feet up on the top. He was enjoying his new found power and basking in his self-importance. Leaning back in his chair, Norm Dinton was the very picture of a pompous man.

Dinton lazily turned his eyes toward the door and listened as he heard the shuffling of feet outside of it. Without a warning the door suddenly swung open and crashed hard against the wall, the violent action almost sent him hurtling backwards out of the chair, but he caught the desk's edge with his fingertips. Dinton's face drained to a deathly pallor as Willard Vaughn stormed through the door. With his jaws unhinged and his mouth hanging open he sat transfixed in his chair, unable to move.

Vaughn's hard blue eyes bore a hole into Dinton's stunned face. "Get the hell out of my chair!"

Dinton could only stare in shock at the man who he was so certain was dead. Vaughn grabbed Dinton's boots and shoved him backwards causing him to slam hard against the wall in a tangle of legs, chair, and flying papers. Coming around the desk, Vaughn grabbed him by the collar and jerked him out from behind the desk. The move shot pain through his back, but he didn't care.

His rage flared as he roared at the dumbstruck lawman. "I've got two bullet holes in my back from your pal Harper Sloan. Did you send him after me? Did you *think* he killed me?"

Dinton shook his head, his mouth still hanging open. "I ... I thought you were dead," he managed to squeak out a whisper.

"I'll bet you did. Where's McCloud?"

"In the back."

Pulling his gun, Vaughn pointed it between Dinton's eyes and thumbed back the hammer. A cry escaped Dinton's lips as he began to tremble, convinced that he was about to be killed. Vaughn held the gun steady as he debated whether to pull the trigger or not. Finally he hissed, "Drop your pistol."

With a trembling hand, Dinton carefully slid the gun from his holster and dropped it on the floor.

"Now, open that door and go in."

Dinton opened the door to the cell area. Vaughn shoved him hard against the bars. Opening a cell door he grabbed Dinton by the collar and threw him inside the cell, sprawling him out on the floor. Slamming the door shut in a resounding clang of steel-on-steel, he turned the key and locked it.

Two cells down, Devon and Trig watched the show with amusement. Vaughn walked up to them and looked them over. "You know Parker; I figured that you'd end up behind bars, but not McCloud."

"Not me Marshal," Trig grinned, "I'm a changed man."

Devon chuckled, "You look pretty good for a dead man Willard."

Vaughn tossed an angry glance toward Dinton. "I'm sure it's a surprise to quite a few people. So, what did you boys do to get yourselves in here?"

Dinton shouted from down the cell row, "They stole cattle."

"Stole cattle?" Vaughn shouted back at him, "Why would they steal cattle? They own more cattle then you've ever seen, you damn idiot."

"They stole Charles Sampson's cattle, them and that Richards fellow."

"What!" Vaughn roared, "You fool, they bought every head on that place and I saw the bill of sale myself. Who said that anyway?"

Dinton refused to answer and retreated to the back of the cell.

"I asked you a question. Who? I'll beat it out of you if I have to and love every minute of it."

Dinton's voice came out weak, "Harper Sloan."

"Harper Sloan!" Vaughn's rage-filled voiced echoed in the room. "You arrested two men on the accusation of a criminal?"

Marching over to the front of the cell with Dinton cowering in the back against the wall Vaughn glared at him. "Let me tell you something about who is under arrest around here. You are! You're under arrest for false arrest, consorting with known criminals, and attempted murder of a peace officer."

"Attempted murder? I never murdered anyone."

"Me, you idiot. You sent Sloan after me."

"I never did that."

"You're the only one who knew where I was going and you've proven yourself to be a friend of Sloan's. Now shut up, if I hear another word out of you I'm going to save the taxpayers the price of a trial."

At this point Jonah walked into the room and stood in front of the cell facing Devon. He shook his head as if in pity, "I feared you'd come to this Devon. A wild young buck, I tried to teach you wisdom, steer you right, but oh no, you had to go off and lead a life of crime."

Devon grinned at Jonah, "You old coot, you going to let us out of this cage or not?"

Jonah looked at Vaughn with mock seriousness, "What do you think Willard, should we give these two outlaws a chance to make honest men of themselves?"

Vaughn looked from Jonah to the two men in the cell and let out a sigh. "Mister Welsh here thinks you should get another chance." Turning the key in the cell door he opened it. "Come on out boys."

Devon walked up to Jonah, "Mister! Folks call you *Mister* Welsh now?"

With a grin Jonah pulled a cigar out of the breast pocket of his coat, struck a match and lit it. "If you recall McCloud, at our last meeting, that I told you the next time you saw me I'd be smoking a dollar cigar. Well, look at me smoking a dollar cigar!"

Devon laughed out loud, "I take it you found your mother lode?"

"Well, it's not a mother lode, but its worth a lot of money."

"You planning to share like your mother taught you to?"

Reaching into his pocket again Jonah produced three more cigars, handing one to each of them he blew out a cloud of smoke. "Never let it be said that Jonah Welsh wouldn't share with his friends."

Vaughn motioned for them to go out into the main office. As the men filed out into the office, he closed the door leaving Dinton alone in the cell. The men turned to face him.

Vaughn tossed the keys on the desk. "Is Sloan in Drewsey?"

Devon's face turned serious. "Yes, he's got a bunch of locals and his own gang trying to run Brian Richards off his place. We can't figure out why, it supposedly has something to do with his getting even for Sampson."

Vaughn shook his head, "It has more to do with it than that. At Sampson's trial I learned an interesting bit of information, it seems Charlie's name isn't Sampson at all, it's Sloan."

"What? Sampson is a Sloan?"

"Harper Sloan's brother, but the best I could gather was that they hated each other. Seems Charlie rode with Harper and Jackson, but they had a falling out. Where it all connects is the mystery."

Devon looked at Trig, "We need to get back there fast."

Before Trig could answer, Hack walked through the open door. Trig laughed, "Little brother what took you so long?"

Hack looked from one face to the other stopping on Vaughn's. "Pleased to see you alive Marshal."

Vaughn grinned, "Pleased to be alive."

Then looking back at his brother Hack added, "I tracked you all the way from where we found your guns, which I did bring with me if you want them. Seems you didn't need me after all."

"Of course we want them and we do need you. You ready for another long ride back?"

"You bet, let's go and finish Sloan off."

Devon looked at Vaughn, "You coming, Marshal?"

"I want to, but I need to guard my prisoner until I can find another man."

"I'll watch him," Jonah volunteered. "You go get Harper Sloan, I'll watch this."

Putting his hand out to his old friend Devon smiled. "Thanks partner, it sure was good to see you again. I've got a wife now, and a good place, you come and see us."

"Congratulations son, you're doing real well and I *will* come to see you, I promise."

Turning around, Devon looked at the men. "Like Hack said, let's go finish Sloan and his outfit off once and for all.

Chapter 17

There was a strange feeling that hung over the town. Harper Sloan kept twisting around in his saddle trying to put a finger on it. He made a face and glanced over to Jackson riding casually next to him. "You feel something funny about this place today?"

Jackson shrugged, "Not really, same old town we left."

"No, it's not. It's too quiet, something happened while we were gone. Let's go find the rest of the boys; I want to know what it was."

Approaching the saloon Sloan pointed at it. "Knolls' horse isn't there. That drunk's always in the saloon, and I don't recognize any of them other horses either. There's always someone from that local bunch in there."

Angling their horses toward the hitch rail in front of the saloon, the two outlaws pulled to a stop and stepped out of their saddles. Sloan stood in the street and looked around. "It's not right."

Jackson gave him an annoyed look, "What did you expect, a brass band?"

"I expected to see those locals here waiting," Sloan snapped back.

"They're ranchers; they can't spend all day hanging around the bar or waiting on you."

"Those haywire outfits?" Sloan laughed sarcastically, "There isn't a cattleman in the bunch. Why do you think it was so easy to pull them into this? They had nothing better to do but feel sorry for themselves."

Jackson shrugged, "I guess that's why Charlie was able to hide here and get to be such a big man; no one realized he didn't know anything about cattle."

Sloan turned a cold glare on his partner. "Charlie owes me, and I intend to collect. He *thought* he could hide behind being a big cattleman, but like everything else he ever did he balled it up. He didn't have the slightest idea what he was doing, so like always, he tried to steal someone else's lot and it got him."

Jackson tossed a quick sidelong glance at Sloan. "Just like we're doing now."

Sloan's face turned red as he started to shake with rage. "That Englishman has what belongs to me and I want it!"

"*Me?*" Jackson's eyes narrowed as he turned slightly to face Sloan. "I thought it belonged to *us*. I was there too, or did you just forget that part? We're *all* here taking a big chance on getting killed and it's all for *you*?"

"I didn't mean it that way."

Jackson squared around to face Sloan. "I think you did, I think you meant it exactly that way. You're using these idiots to fight your fight for you and we're all here in case they can't do it, so you're using us too. When we take on Richards' guns will you be that last man standing?"

The red in Sloan's face and neck deepened as he glowered at Jackson.

Jackson's anger was up and he went on. "You want to talk about funny feelings, Harp? I have a funny feeling this whole thing has been set up just for you. Here's another one since we're talking about it. You've bit off way more than you can chew with this. You killed a Marshal and that puts a rope around all our necks. Richards is stronger than we expected and shooting Raven didn't stop them, it just made them fighting mad. Getting McCloud and Parker out of here won't help either. Now, after all that, I find out it's just for *you*, what's in this for the rest of us? We can't beat this outfit, so why should we get killed to make *you* rich?"

"I think your guts have run out Jackson and you want to use me for your excuse to turn your tail and run."

"I know when I see four aces sitting up in front of the dealer and I've got a pair of deuces I get out of the game."

Sloan moved in close to Jackson and snarled in his face, "Then fold your yellow hand and run."

Jackson took a step back and put his hand down on the butt of his Colt. Sloan did the same. The sound of moving boots held them up but neither man dared to shift his eyes to look. Sloan's five men slowed their walk and approached carefully, it was obvious to them that a deadly situation was at hand with their leader and Jackson.

Lowering his hand, Sloan took a step back and looked at the men. The first thing he saw was one man with a wrapped and splinted arm, another with black eyes and a swollen nose, and a third with half a raw ear. "What happened to the three of you?"

The wounded men looked at the ground and nervously shuffled their feet in the dirt. Pulling at his splinted arm the one spoke timidly, "We had a run-in with Richards' men."

"So, what happened?"

The men all looked at each other as if seeking approval for the story. "They came in here looking for trouble and we took care of it, but we got chewed up a little ourselves."

A loud roar of laughter from the street made the men turn to see who it was. A rider they didn't recognize had stopped his horse next to the group and sat in the saddle with an amused look. "That's the biggest load of bull I've ever heard. Your bully-boys here tried to take on Brian Richards' man, you know, the *Butler*, he shot them two and just beat the ears off him."

Sloan's glare turned on the stranger and then back to the man with the splinted arm. The rider laughed louder, "Ask them about your pal Farley Knolls while you're at it. If I were you Sloan, I'd be getting as far away from here as I could." Still laughing the rider touched spurs to his horse and rode on down the street.

With his jaws clenched, Sloan stomped off into the saloon. Grabbing a bottle off the bar he went to his usual table and sat down hard. Pulling the cork out of the bottle he angrily threw it across the room bouncing it off the wall. Putting the bottle to his lips he gulped a large mouthful and slammed the bottle back on the table.

"Tell me about Knolls and whatever that loud mouth was talking about."

The men all looked at each other until Sloan slammed his fist on the table, "Tell me!"

One of the men volunteered the answer, "The Englishman came in looking for you, and Knolls braced him."

"And?"

"Richards outdrew him and shot him dead."

Sloan took another long drink from the bottle. "I thought Knolls was supposed to be some kind of gunfighter."

The man shrugged, "I don't know, I guess he was all talk."

"I was counting on that blowhard to take Richards, not get killed by him. Go get Chic Took and the rest of Knolls' followers, tell them I want to talk to them. We finally got rid of McCloud and

Parker and I don't want to lose this chance. Without his gunmen to side him, we can put an end to Richards right now."

Silence fell over the men again. Sloan looked at them, his eyes smoldering with hate and rage. "Now what?"

"Took and his boys went out to Richards' place to take care of him for killing Knolls." The man stopped talking and looked at his friends.

Sloan pushed his fists into the table top and came to his feet. Bending over it he snarled in the man's face, "Tell me the darn story!"

"They got wiped out."

"Every one of them?"

"All but one, who came back in all beat up with a rope burn around his neck. He told us what happened and then left town."

Throwing himself back into the chair, Sloan grabbed the back of his shoulder with his hand and tipped his head back. Growling with rage he glared at the ceiling. "I leave for a couple of days and the whole plan goes to pieces."

Letting out a long exasperated sigh he concluded, "We'll just finish him off ourselves then."

The men once again turned silent and fidgeted nervously. Sloan brought his head back down and glared at them. "What now? You scared?"

Jackson was slumped in a chair to Sloan's right, "I think nobody wants to ride out there and get shot to pieces."

"I already know where you stand."

The only part of Jackson that moved was his eyes and they could have killed Harper Sloan where he sat.

The tension between Sloan and Jackson made the men even more nervous. There had always been a strong partnership between the two men, but now it had degenerated into something they recognized all too well. These were two men ready to kill each other. They had always known Travis Jackson to have a level head and if he was giving Sloan the killing eye something had caused that bad blood and they doubted that the blame lay with Jackson.

Sloan finally moved his eyes from Jackson's and focused on the group as a whole. "We ride out to Richards' tomorrow morning."

"Have him come here instead."

Sloan glared back at Jackson, "Why?"

"Get him out of his own yard. Even a dog fights better in his own home, don't give him the advantage. Call him out, but make him come to us."

Sloan paused to mull the idea over. Even in his agitated state he could sense the reasoning in the idea. Looking at the man with the bruised face he gave him an order. "Tell Richards to meet us at the cattle pens tomorrow afternoon and we'll settle this once and for all."

"What if he doesn't want to come?"

"Tell him if he doesn't want his place ground into the dirt and his men wiped out he'd better come. Tell him I think he's too gutless to face me. That ought to get him here."

The man hesitated and shifted his eyes to those around him. He didn't want any more to do with Richards or any of his outfit. Returning his gaze to Sloan he saw the anger in his eyes and decided that it was safer to face Richards than Sloan. He nodded slightly and headed for the door.

Picking up the bottle, Sloan took another long drink from it. Slamming the bottle back down he growled at the men in front of him. "Now get out of here, but be at the pens tomorrow."

Slowly the four men drifted away from their leader. They had lost their taste for the fight, but they had followed Harper Sloan too long to desert him now. Reputations were on the line and their fear of being branded as cowards was greater than their fear of buying a bullet from one of Brian Richards' fighting men.

The sour look on Sloan's face held as he watched the men drift out the door. When they had gone he turned toward Jackson, "I thought you didn't want to help."

"I want us to come out of this alive, charging his house will get us all killed. If he comes here we might have a chance." Jackson got up out of his chair.

Sloan looked up at him. "Where you going?"

"Anywhere away from you."

"So you're running then."

"No, I'll be at the pens, then we're through."

"You're breaking up the partnership because we had an argument?"

Jackson's expression revealed his new found contempt for Sloan. "I figure I owe you this one last time, I'll side you tomorrow, but no man calls me yellow and lives – or stays my friend."

He studied Sloan's face and decided he looked just like his brother. "You know something Sloan? You hated Charlie, hated him for years, and I don't blame you after the trick he pulled. He cheated both of us Harp; not just you, but right now I don't see a lick of difference between you and him."

Sloan sat like he was nailed to the chair. He couldn't believe that he was losing his partner after more than twenty years of riding together. He realized that he had run his mouth once too often and it had cost him, but he was too proud to apologize.

"Fine, go, and don't bother showing up tomorrow."

"Oh I'll be there, if for no other reason than to see what happens to you. If Richards doesn't kill you, I might." With that, Jackson walked a straight line to the saloon door and out.

With Jackson's words echoing in his ears Sloan sat stunned. He had no use for any man on earth and would just as soon gun someone down as look at him, but Travis Jackson had been his friend forever, the only one he had. Taking another drink from the bottle, he set it down and began to justify himself. He decided that Jackson had indeed turned yellow on him and he was better off without him. If the man couldn't take the truth then to the hell with him, besides now he didn't have to split anything with him.

The whiskey was taking its effect on him, his head was starting to swim and his senses were growing dull. It was a moment before he realized that a man was standing across the table from him. His first thought was that Jackson had come crawling back to get back on his good side again. Staring up at the man, it was another moment before what his eyes took in became recognition. It was Mel Johns in front of him; he felt a sudden surge of disappointment.

"What do you want, Johns?"

Mel Johns felt a wave of fear come over him and then he took a good hard look at the drunken outlaw sitting in front of him and realized there was nothing there to fear, Harper Sloan was nothing. "I came to talk to you."

"I don't want to talk, be at the pens tomorrow." Sloan's voice was slow and slurred.

"Pens? What about the pens?"

"We're going to kill that Englishman there tomorrow."

"Okay, I'll be there ...."

"Good man Johns, I knew I could count on you."

"You didn't let me finish. I'll be there ... to back Richards."

Sloan's head swayed on his shoulders as he tried to focus on the man in front of him. "You lose your nerve too?"

Johns' voice reflected pride in himself, yet was thick with contempt for the outlaw. "No, I finally found it. You shot a friend of mine. Sam Raven is on thin ice right now and I helped put him there. If I had found my nerve sooner, I'd have stood up to you and Farley Knolls and Sam would be up right now. I lost a good friend siding a worthless pile of horse manure like you and now its time to right it."

"Who says I shot Raven?"

"It doesn't take much imagination to figure that one out. He makes a fool out of you by giving you a good beating and then he ends up shot in the back by a coward. Not much of a mystery there."

Sloan glared at Johns, his eyes whiskey dulled. "You be there Johns and you can die with the rest of 'em."

Johns let out a laugh that even surprised him, "If anyone dies tomorrow it'll be you and good riddance to you too."

Chapter 18

Sloan's messenger rode in cautiously. He could see the house Brian Richards lived in and make out the activity of men all around it. He held no doubts that this outfit was ready to blow any man out of the saddle who even resembled a problem. He had come to Drewsey cocky and ready for the profit he'd get from driving this Englishman out, it seemed like an easy thing, but it had proven to be anything but easy.

He pulled his horse up and studied the place from a safe distance. It was a hot day with a dry desert wind blowing; the sweat that ran down his face and back and soaked his shirt was from more than the heat. He was scared, flat scared, he'd never admit it to a living soul, but Brian Richards and his men scared him. He had been witness to the fighting ability of McCloud and Raven, even that butler of his could fight. Then, to top it off, they go and wipe out Took and his boys. Only a fool like Sloan wouldn't be afraid. Now, he was supposed to ride right into that hornet's nest. He didn't like it one bit.

Nudging his horse forward, he made his way down the hill. As the house drew nearer the sweat was pouring out of every pore in his body. He braced himself for the bullet he knew was coming any minute. He could make out the details of the house before anyone noticed him and then they saw him. He braced again as men came on the run to meet him. Holding his hands out to his sides and just letting the horse walk, he hoped they wouldn't shoot. He found himself wishing he had a white flag, a very big white flag. Squeezing his knees into the horse's sides, the sorrel came to a stop.

Bill Anthony broke from the half-dozen men and approached the rider. The outlaw stayed in the saddle with his hands outstretched. Bill stopped a few feet in front of him. "You're one of Sloan's men, what do you want?"

"I ain't lookin' for trouble mister; I've just come to deliver a message."

"Then spit it out."

"I'm supposed to give it to the Englishman."

Richards appeared on the house porch and looked at the rider. "Here I am. What is your message?"

"Now, don't shoot me or anything, I'm just telling you what Harper Sloan told me to. He said that he wants you to meet him at the cattle pens north of town tomorrow afternoon." He decided not to tell Richards the part about him being gutless.

"Why?"

"I reckon he wants a final showdown with you."

Richards studied the man without answering as his men turned to watch him for a reaction or answer. They were ready to ride that minute for Drewsey and have at it with Sloan and his boys, but it all depended on their boss' answer.

"Tell him I will be there."

Bill turned back around and looked up at the outlaw. "You've delivered your message and you've got your answer; now get off this ranch."

With his hands still outstretched he nodded, "I'll tell him. Do you boys mind if I pickup my reins and turn this horse around?"

"Go ahead," Bill eyed him suspiciously, "but if you come up with anything except reins, you're dead."

"Don't worry, I'm no fool."

Slowly the outlaw gathered the reins and pulled the horse's head around and touched spurs to him. He moved out at a walk and then broke into a lope, putting the ranch behind him as fast as he could.

Bill watched him until he was out of sight and then looked back over his shoulder. "Do you think that's a good idea Mister Richards, meeting Sloan's gang on their terms?"

"I won't have them attacking this place again and burning down the rest of our buildings. I will meet him away from here and finish this foul business once and for all."

Turning completely around Bill looked squarely at Richards. "By 'I' you mean *we* don't you?"

"No Bill, I mean exactly what I said. *I* will face them. Enough men have been injured fighting for me. It is my fight and I will finish it."

Bill Anthony's face turned hard as he hunted for the exact words he wanted to say. "Mister Richards, it's not my place to argue with your decisions and you can fire me for it if you want, but I aim to speak my mind here. I don't think you completely understand our way of thinking. Out in this country when a man rides for another man, takes his pay and eats his grub, he does more than take up a place at the supper table, he rides for the brand. Whatever happens to that brand happens to each man riding for it. You're a good man Mister Richards, and you've always treated every one of us fair and square. Sam Raven was a good friend to all of us and we intend to make his being shot by Sloan's outfit right. You can order us to stay, but we'll come anyway, every last one of us. It's not just *your* fight Mister Richards. This fight belongs to all of us and we intend to stand behind you and the brand and fight for it."

Richards stood stone still as the words sunk into his mind. He had no response for such a code of honor or loyalty. These cowboys were truly unique men. He watched the other men move up to stand beside Bill.

Frank Perry crossed his arms and looked his boss in the eye. "Bill pretty much said it, don't try leaving without us."

The lump that stuck in Richards' throat refused to go down. He wanted to say something to offer his thanks for their loyalty, however he knew these men needed no thanks and expected none, it was their code. A code that their existence revolved around, it wasn't merely words but the very breath they breathed, and no man alive could sway them from it for fear or money. He felt his chest swell with pride to be among such men.

Coughing to clear his throat he nodded, "Of course, I meant *we*." Then pausing, he saw the glow come on each man's face. "However, some of you will have to stay. This entire arrangement could be a trap to draw us all away from the ranch. If we all leave they could be waiting out there to charge in and finish the job."

The men looked at each other and spoke among themselves to the effect that this was a valid point and some of them would have to stay. It was agreed that Bill and Frank would ride with Richards to meet Sloan.

Bill turned his attention back to Richards. "Frank and I will go with you and the rest of the men will stay here and guard the place." Then he grinned, "Besides, three Juniper men is more than a match for that crowd."

"Very good, the three of us will ride in together."

Morning found the men up before daylight going about their usual ranch duties. The afternoon was several hours away and viewed with a mix of anticipation for the fight, and hope for an end to the trouble. However, anxiety that Brian Richards could be killed overshadowed everything. Bill and Frank had agreed that if Richards was killed by Sloan, they would shoot the entire gang to doll rags, none would be allowed to ride away.

Richards joined the men for the noon meal in the chuckhouse. Conversation was light as the men ate in silence, each in his own thoughts. Richards was the first to rise from his seat, picking up his plate and fork he dropped them in the wash basin of water and turned for the door. George watched him without speaking while Bill and Frank followed suit.

Before Richards reached the door, Kenny Weaver struggled to his feet, leaning heavily on his crutch he moved to block Richards' way. The big man filled the doorway as he came to a stop. Putting his hand out he looked his boss in the eye. "You come back now."

Richards took his hand, "I have every intention to."

Weaver reached back and opened the door; cussing the crutch under his breath, he left the room. The rest of the men watched in silence as the three followed him out. Behind them came the shuffling of boots on the wood floor. As they made their way to the corral, the men who were remaining at the ranch headed for the bunkhouse to collect their rifles.

The three men worked in silence as they caught up their horses and tacked them out. They knew what lay ahead of them and no words were needed. It had come down to this, a final confrontation that would end the situation once and for all. Either they would die or Sloan and his gang would, but today there was going to be blood on the ground.

Richards rode out first. As they passed the bunkhouse, he looked over to see Kenny Weaver in front of it. He was sitting in a chair against the wall, his crutch on the ground and a Winchester across his knees. He waved as they rode by, Richards returned it.

The sound of a horse coming up behind them caused all three to turn around to look. Henry was making his way toward them. They stopped and watched him approach. Henry smiled at Richards, "Did you think I would not come to back you? That you could so easily leave me behind?"

Richards smiled, "Of course not, my old friend."

The four rode in silence, like men going off to war. Richards studied the scene around him; it struck him as interesting how a man takes so much for granted, the sights, smells, and sounds. This high desert country was such a contrast to his native land of thick green grass carpets and rainy days. It was different, but he loved it here. The strong scent of sage and juniper that swirled in the breeze, eagles soaring overheard, and the startling explosions of sage hens from underfoot. He wondered if he would be riding back this way again.

He had faced death many times over and had always come out on the winning end. He recalled the time Albert Chaney had risked his life to stay with him, the memory still moved him. Albert was ten years older than him and had taken him under his wing and taught him how to survive in war. A strong and lasting bond of friendship had formed, more like brothers than comrades. He had used the lessons Albert taught him many times and they had kept him alive, he would use those lessons again today. Would he be riding back to the Juniper? He knew he would be.

Thinking deep has a way of making the minutes and hours fly by. Richards' mind came back to the task at hand when the barking of a dog brought him abruptly up to attention. He swept the town with his eyes and found that little had changed in the face of the events that had taken place between him and those who wanted him out. Then again, this was a town made up of rough men from every walk of life, little would be made here of men fighting be it fists or guns.

Passing through the town, he could make out the cattle pens nestled in the sage. Some of the plants were big enough to hide a man and blocked out some of the view, but not so much that he couldn't make out several horses and men standing in front of the pen rails. Richards suddenly realized that with all the injury and damage Harper Sloan was responsible for he had yet to actually meet the man. He had no idea which one of the men in front of the pens was Sloan.

As he continued riding directly for the cluster of men, Bill and Frank pulled out their rifles and fanned out to his either side to flank him and better their odds when this came down to shooting. Stopping his horse a hundred paces from the outlaws, Richards studied their positioning. There were seven men all standing within an arm's reach of each other. The man standing in the center of them wore a heavy black mustache and the hair coming out from under his hat was equally as black. The cold hard eyes peering out from under the hat's brim could only belong to one man; this had to be Harper Sloan.

Slowly, like a man without a care in the world, Richards dismounted. Peeling off his riding jacket he tossed it over the saddlehorn, turning his gunside to the horse to hide his action he slid the .41 up a bit in the holster to make sure it was clear. Dropping his reins on the ground, he advanced toward the black haired man. His two men did the same, coming in from his right and left.

Forty feet from the outlaws Richards stopped. "I take it you are Harper Sloan?"

Sloan hooked his thumbs under his belt buckle and struck a pose meant to intimidate. "That's me. I see you made it; I see you also brought your butler along."

Henry dismounted and took several steps to Richards' right. He never said a word, just opened his coat to reveal the pistol on his hip.

Sloan sneered, "I was betting you'd be half way back to England by now."

"Does this look like England to you?"

"Nope, and I intend to keep it that way. You need to leave and give me back my property."

"Your property? I don't recall your name being connected with this property when I purchased and finalized the deed with the bank. I am sure it would have come up in the proceedings."

"That's the whole problem your *Lordship*, my name was never on it because Charlie bought it with money he stole from me."

Travis Jackson was standing several feet to Sloan's left; he tossed him an angry glare and held it on him. Sloan never moved his head, but he could feel his former partner's hate.

Richards continued to hold his best poker face and refused to show emotion, he had no intention of sending his enemy any signals as to his coming actions. "That is something you will have to take up with Charlie, you can find him in the State Penitentiary."

"I know exactly where Charlie is and he can stay there, or in hell for all I care. It doesn't matter to me; I just want what's mine."

"Well Mister Sloan, you are not going to get it."

Shifting his position, Sloan spread his feet a shoulder's width apart and hovered his right hand over his Colt. "You see *Mister* Richards, that's where you're wrong. I intend to take claim to my property right now."

Bill and Frank cocked back the hammers on their rifles, shouldered them and took aim on the men to either side of Sloan. The action was caught by those siding Sloan and they knew then they would all die.

The outlaw's eyes suddenly shifted off Richards to something coming up behind him. Richards could see Sloan's expression change to a look of confusion as he tried to keep an eye on him and at the same time figure out what was coming toward his back. Then the sound of sagebrush scratching on leather and the movement of horses' hooves came to him. He wondered if Sloan's local friends had come to join him for the final killing. His curiosity was aroused but he didn't dare take his eyes off of Sloan to see.

As the sound came along side of him and then passed to move in front he recognized Israel Dodd and Mel Johns with another man. The three riders came up on Sloan's right and pulled their horses to a stop.

Sloan turned his head slightly to take in the riders. "I see you made it Johns."

Mel Johns looked down on the outlaw. "You recall what I told you yesterday?"

Sloan stared at him, "Some."

"Probably not, you were pretty drunk. I told you I'd be here alright ... to back Richards."

The announcement shocked Richards, the last time he saw Johns he was with the group that came to run him off, but he knew that Israel Dodd was on his side. Now, Johns was declaring his support for him. It was confusing, but welcome.

The men standing with Sloan began to fidget nervously; seven against one was their kind of odds. Then it turned out to be seven against four, with the two Juniper foremen already leveling rifles on them and they had already seen what the *Butler* could do. Now, it was even, some of them were sure to be killed if lead started flying. They began to wonder if Harper Sloan was worth it.

Israel Dodd stepped out of the saddle swinging a double barreled shotgun across the crook of his right arm. He stepped in next to the line of outlaws. Spitting a stream of tobacco juice on the ground he grinned. "I figure I can cut most of you in half from here."

Glancing up at the man mounted next to him Dodd chuckled, "What do you think Pat, should I use both barrels at once or just one and see what's left?"

Pat Lyons leaned forward resting his forearm on his saddlehorn. "That's a tough one Israel, both ideas sound good. Maybe they ain't worth wasting two shells when one will do the trick."

The outlaws all jumped when Dodd leveled the shotgun at them and thumbed back both hammers. "I need to think about it, so for right now you boys just march on into that open pen right there." Gesturing with the gun to an open gate on their left he added, "Oh, and drop them guns before you go in and don't be gettin' funny with 'em either."

The five men carefully lifted the guns from their holsters and dropped them in the sand. Holding their hands out clear of their bodies they walked toward the pen.

Johns rode up and herded them in, turning in the saddle he pointed his pistol at Jackson. "You too, drop that gun and get in with them."

Obeying without question, Jackson followed the others into the pen. Johns moved his horse in close and pushed the gate shut with his foot. Dodd walked up next to him still holding the shotgun on them.

Dodd lowered the hammers on the shotgun. "There you go Sloan, just the two of you. Brian can do whatever he pleases from here."

Sloan didn't care for the turn of events; he wanted a swift end to the whole affair so he could move in and start counting his money. He had shifted around to watch the disarming of his men, at every turn he had been stopped and he was tired of it. He knew it was impossible to win anything now; even if he killed Richards, his friends would kill him.

Turning back to face Richards, Sloan stood stone silent while Richards faced him, never moving. The men studied the nerve of the other and neither wavered, then without a wasted movement Harper Sloan went for his gun.

Richards had anticipated the move. He could see the man had nerve and was going to eventually pull the gun. He felt his hand slap down on the smooth hardwood grips of the .41, felt its weight, and brought it up and forward. The shots popped like river ice at thirty below, one rolling over the other. The reports echoed back to the town, two, four, and then a final fifth shot and the desert returned to silence.

Chapter 19

Abby was standing in front of the schoolhouse introducing Marie to the two men who had organized the school when she heard the gunfire. With a start she swung around to look at Marie. "That wasn't target practice or huntin', that was a gunfight."

Running out into the street she looked all around. She wasn't sure why the shooting had upset her so badly, she had heard plenty of shooting around town, but this carried the knell of death with it.

Katy came running from the general store and joined her mother in the street. "Where was that?"

"I don't know, but it's Brian . . . I just know it's Brian."

Men began running out of the buildings headed for the cattle holding pens outside of town. Katy strained her eyes to see through the strong afternoon sun. "Ma, the pens, I see a bunch of men and horses down by the pens."

Marie remained standing with the two men, her face a picture of worry and confusion. She shouted toward Abby, "What was that shooting?"

"I don't know, something seems to have happened over there. You stay put."

Walking as fast as she could, Abby made her way through the sage. Men ran past her, but she kept going. Katy stayed beside her, catching the aging woman each time she tripped over a sage root. Abby was almost crying as she mumbled prayers for Brian's life to be spared.

"Ma," Katy spoke between gasps for breath, "It's probably just some cowboys settling an argument."

"No, it's Brian, I know it. Lord, I hope he's not dead."

As the two women drew closer, they could make out a group of men closed up in a pen with a man standing in front of them with a gun. Another was sprawled out on the ground, while several other men were bent over something on the ground.

Pushing past the onlookers, Abby recognized Bill and Frank bent over a man on the ground, Pat Lyons stood over them. Then her fears were realized as she saw that Brian was the man lying in the dirt, his eyes looking up and blinking.

Dropping down on her knees next to him the old woman sobbed. Frank moved over to give her some room. Richards looked up at her and tried to smile, "I thought I was going to be the last man standing, but I see we are both down."

Henry had Richards' shirt torn open and was holding a wad of bandanas down on a wound just below the ribcage while the blood oozed out under it. He looked at Katy, grimaced and whispered, "I don't know how bad it is. The bullet never came out."

Another minute passed before men began shouting to make a clear path for the doctor. Doctor James pushed his way between the men and lifted the makeshift bandage from the wound. Opening his bag he pulled out some clean cloths and wiped the blood away from the wound. Sliding his hand under Richards' back he felt for the exit wound and found none. Removing a long thin metal tool from the bag he gingerly slid it into the bullet hole. Richards groaned and clenched his teeth. The tool went into the wound a couple of inches and stopped. Pulling the tool back out he pressed the cloths down on the wound.

Looking up he shouted, "Some of you men get him to my office quick."

Several men clasped their hands together to make a carrier while others picked Richards up and laid him on their arms. Hurriedly they headed back to town.

James looked at the worried faces in front of him. "The bullet's still in there and that could be good, if it had gone through he'd be dead. At this time there seems to be no vital organs hit." Putting a comforting hand on Abby's shoulder he smiled, "He'll live."

Katy hugged her mother as they both cried in relief. Katy wiped her eyes and looked at Bill and Frank. "What went on here?"

Frank pointed at the pen still holding Sloan's men. "They sent word to Mister Richards that Sloan wanted to meet him here for a final showdown. He was going to come alone, but we wouldn't let him. We got here and then Israel, Mel, and Pat showed up to side us. It came down to Brian and Sloan." Half turning around he gestured toward Harper Sloan lying dead behind them. "You can see how that came out."

"It would have been a lot worse," Bill broke in, "if Israel hadn't cut the odds down. He leveled his twelve gauge on that crew and herded 'em into the pen like cattle. That brought it down to just the two of them. For a minute there I thought Sloan was going to back down, and then all of a sudden he had his gun out. Brian actually hit him first, but he didn't go down."

The sound of new movement in the sagebrush brought Katy's attention to it. She stifled a cry as she turned and looked into her husband's face. Reaching out his arms to her Katy jumped into them. She clung tightly to him refusing to let go while the tears flowed freely.

Reluctantly she let go and stepped back. "What happened to you?"

"It's a long story; we'll talk about it later."

"Devon, Brian's been shot."

Devon's eyes flashed with fear, "Where is he?"

"They took him to the Doctor's house; he said Brian will be okay though."

The relief flooded Devon's face as he nodded his understanding. Looking past Katy he saw the body of Harper Sloan, his gun lying beside his open hand. Tipping his chin toward the body, "Brian do that?"

"According to Bill and Frank he did, they had a shootout."

"It was something to see Devon." Bill walked up to Devon and slapped him on the back. "Richards has more guts than any ten men I've ever met. He stood up there going shot for shot with Sloan, he nailed Sloan once, but he wouldn't go down. Then we saw the bullet hit Richards and he fell, I was making ready to shoot Sloan myself when the boss, while on the ground, lifted his gun and fired one last shot and Sloan went down like a sack of feed."

Supported by Frank, Abby made her way to Devon. She threw her arms around him while Frank shook his hand. "It's good to see you alive Devon."

"Good to *be* alive," Devon smiled while returning Abby's hug. Gesturing with his head over his shoulder he added, "Speaking of being alive, look who we found."

They all looked behind Devon. Trig and Hack were standing with Dodd laughing and joking about the corralled outlaws, then they made out the man standing next them. Abby squinted her eyes, "Vaughn? Is that Willard Vaughn?"

Devon chuckled, "In the flesh. He's part of the long story, too."

As a group they made their way to the pen and the men in front of it. Abby walked up to Trig and Hack and looked up at them. "Well, if you two ain't a pair to draw to."

Trig grinned, "Can't whip a Parker, let alone two." Then he winked at Katy, "And then throw a McCloud in on top of it."

Turning toward Vaughn, Abby put out her hand. "Glad to see you Marshal, we heard that you had been killed."

Shaking her hand he smiled and tipped his hat. "This outfit tried, but a man who turned out to be a friend of Devon's found me and got me patched up."

Devon pointed at the outlaws, "What are you going to do with them. Can't trail the whole herd back to Baker City."

Vaughn glared at the men behind the corral rails. "No, I can't and I sure don't want to just let them go either."

Dodd grinned, "We could just hang the lot of them right here."

Vaughn stepped up to the rails and glared at the outlaws. "What do you boys think about that? Do something worthwhile for once in your lives and save the taxpayers the cost of putting up with you, just hang you here? Personally, I like the idea."

There was no reply from the six men only shocked faces and the nervous shuffling of feet.

Focusing his attention on Travis Jackson, Vaughn shouted at him. "Jackson get out here."

Reluctantly the outlaw slid between the rails and came up to the Marshal. "Jackson I want some answers, and I'd better get them or I will definitely string you up right here and now."

Jackson nodded, "I had a falling out with Sloan just before this, I'll tell you whatever you want."

"Now, I know Charlie Sampson was really a Sloan, and him and Harper were brothers, but I want to know why he was here going after Brian Richards."

Abby's face fell as she grabbed Vaughn's arm. "Sampson was Harper Sloan's brother?"

"His real name is Charles Sloan; I found that out at the trial. For some reason he came here and changed his name, and that's what I want to know about." Turning his attention back to Jackson he glared at him, "And that's what you're going to tell me."

Jackson nodded, "Charlie is Harp's older brother. At first the gang was just the three of us, Charlie was the leader. We rode together for quite a while, but there was little love between Charlie and Harp, in fact I think they hated each other. One day we held up a stage that was headed into Virginia City. We didn't know it, but that stage had a huge mine payroll on it. Charlie shot the shotgun rider. When we found the money, he killed the driver so no one would know it was us. There was thousands of dollars in those bags. We were pretty excited about it, but Charlie insisted that we split up and hide out until the robbery and killings cooled down. He took the money with him since he was the leader and told us to meet him at a place we had up in the hills west of Reno.

"Harp was dead set against it, but Charlie was a mean one and got his way. Well, you can guess the rest of the story, Charlie never showed up. We had no idea where he went, we tried to find him, but he had just fell in a hole someplace. The best we could figure was that he had run off with the whole load or maybe he'd been killed and the money lost. We worked around Reno for a while, then up into the Rubies, and finally we drifted over to Baker City. Harp never got over what Charlie had done to us.

"It was just by accident that we found out about Charlie. Harp was looking at a newspaper and there was a story about this Charles Sampson being a big cattleman and on trial for trying to kill some widow and steal her place. I made a joke about this Charles being as mean as Charlie and they both having the same name and all. I can still see the look on Harp's face when I said that. He got to believing it was Charlie, so we went to the trial and watched. Sure enough, it was Charlie Sloan, a bunch of years older, and he had changed his name to Sampson, but it was the same man.

"Harp stewed on it over the winter. All he could think about was that Charlie was in prison and there was no way to get at him. We never put the missing money and Charlie's big ranch together until a couple of months ago. That's when we decided to head on down to Drewsey and try to find where the money went. Harp asked around and added up everything he learned, and it was plain that Charlie had used the holdup money to buy his ranch and cattle. Harp went crazy.

"After he calmed down Harp got to figuring that all he had to do was come forward as Charlie's brother and take over the ranch, since Charlie was in prison and all. That is until he found out the Englishman had bought it. That's when he cooked up this idea to get the locals riled up against the Englishman and run him out; if that didn't work we'd run him out ourselves and take over.

"The plan started out pretty good, but we kept running into hitches. Harp had never counted on Trig Parker being on the Englishman's side, the two of them had a history. Trig hated Harp's guts and Harp was scared of him. Then there was McCloud. That's when he got Dinton to arrest them to get them out of the way. He figured it was a clear trail after that, but he didn't count on the ranch crew fighting back, and he sure never figured the Englishman to be as tough as he was. The rest ended today, as you can see." Jackson stopped talking and looked at the hard faces around him.

Vaughn mulled the story over. "That all adds up alright, but why did he try to kill me? I had nothing to do with your problems with Charlie."

"He didn't know if you were onto the connection between him and Charlie. After he got the plan rolling here he didn't want anyone to know that Charlie Sampson was actually Charlie Sloan, so he wanted you dead just in case you did."

"Did Dinton have any part in my getting shot?"

"Yeah, he's the one that set Harp on your trail. He wanted to be the big man in town."

Looking over at Devon Vaughn scowled. "Well, that explains it."

"It does that. So, what are you going to do with this bunch?"

Vaughn looked them over, "Any place we can lock them up while I send off a couple of wires?"

Israel Dodd waved toward the town, "Go on Marshal send your wires, Pat and I'll take care of this pack of coyotes."

Vaughn waved back, "Thanks, and if they try to make a break for it you have my permission to shoot 'em."

As the group headed toward town Dodd called out after Mel Johns, "Mel, you want to stay here with us?"

"No, I've got a friend I need to see."

Israel nodded and waved, "You do that."

The group made their way through the sage, with the men leading their horses walking alongside Abby and Katy. Breaking out of the sage and onto the clear street they continued on to the doctor's house. A crowd of men were gathered outside waiting to hear word of Richards' condition. They parted to allow Devon and his family to the door; opening it they went inside and stood in the front room.

The doctor's wife greeted them. "Peter got the bullet out and found that there was no serious damage done. Mister Richards will need rest and time to recover, but he will be fine."

A surge of relief ran through the group. Devon stepped forward, "Can we see him?"

Mrs. James smiled and gestured for them to follow. "I see no harm in that. The doctor gave him anesthesia and he may be drowsy and not feeling well."

Trig put his hand on Devon's back, "The three of you go in, we'll wait out here."

Opening the door, Mrs. James stepped aside and let them pass her with Abby and Katy going in first. Richards was lying on a table covered with a blanket, his bloody shirt on the floor next to him. He turned his head at their entrance and whispered a greeting, "Excuse me if I don't get up."

Then his eyes slowly shifted past them to Devon. "Devon, you are back, I'm so glad." He closed his eyes and faded into sleep.

Doctor James came in behind them. "He'll sleep off and on like that for a while. The bullet hit a rib, deflected and settled in between two others, nothing vital was damaged and it was a relatively easy surgery. Now, I have someone else you should see."

Leading them down a short hall the doctor opened another door. "Go on in."

Sam Raven opened his eyes and watched the three come in. Doctor James followed them. "He came around this morning, I was going to send word, but then all of this happened, and since you're here anyway you can have the good word now. Sam's past the worst of it."

Excited talk was exchanged as Abby, Katy, and Devon stood next to the bed. Devon looked down on him, "You planning on laying around forever Raven? Some cowpuncher you turned out to be, taking to your bed when there's work to be done."

Sam smiled and winced a bit, his voice barely above a whisper. "If there's work to be done what are you doing here?"

Devon decided that Sam didn't need to know about the afternoon or Richards just yet. "Ah, just in town and heard you were doing better."

"Pete says I'll live."

Abby stepped forward, "You'd better Sam Raven, there's folks here expectin' you back on your feet."

"How goes the battle, Devon?"

"It's over. Harper Sloan is dead."

Sam's eyes reflected satisfaction, "Good. How's Richards?"

"He's fine. In fact he's the one that killed Sloan. There's a lot to tell, but it can wait until you're doing better."

Doctor James came up beside them. "That's right Sam; it's going to take awhile for that lung to heal, the less talking the better."

Getting behind them, the doctor ushered the three out of the room. Trig was standing alone with Mel Johns. Devon looked around, "Where's Hack and Willard?"

"They went to send the telegrams."

Devon then turned his attention to Johns. "Thanks Mel."

Mel Johns hung his head and shook it. "I don't think I'll ever live down the shame."

Devon put his hand out, "You just did."

Looking up, Johns' face was an image of hope as he took Devon's offered hand. "I'd like to see Sam if I could." His eyes pleaded toward the doctor.

Doctor James nodded, "But only for a minute."

"That's all I need."

Johns slowly opened the door and hesitantly stepped into the room. Sam's head turned toward him, his eyes turning unfriendly upon seeing him. Nervously he walked toward the bed. "I came to apologize Sam ... I was a fool."

Sam remained silent and studied the man.

Sam's eyes shifted to look behind him. Devon stepped up beside Johns. "I should tell you Sam. There was a shootout between Brian and Sloan's gang this afternoon."

Sam whispered, "I know, I heard all the commotion."

Devon wasn't surprised. "What you don't know is that Mel came in with Israel and Pat Lyons to side Brian. If they hadn't, we'd be at the graveyard right now burying some good men."

Sam's eyes shifted back to Johns, he studied him for another long minute. "We all make mistakes Mel, but our friends see us through them ... don't they?"

Johns broke into a broad smile, "That's what friends are for and I'm happy to see I haven't lost one of my best." Johns stood still smiling at Sam until Devon tapped his shoulder and indicated that they should leave. Together they turned and left the room.

Devon stopped up short, his mouth dropping open. "Ma?"

Marie McCloud stood in the room with Abby and Katy. Tears rolled down her cheeks as she nodded her head. "Devon." Mother and son rushed to embrace each other.

"Abby and Katy picked me up at the stage stop the day after you disappeared; we were all so worried about you."

Abby stepped up to them. "Not your ma Devon, she said they couldn't stop a McCloud and she was right."

"I was with Abby, meeting the school people when all the shooting happened."

"Have you met Brian yet Ma?" Devon's voice was hesitant.

"Yes, he is a very nice man."

"He's English, you know."

"I know, but isn't it time we put all that behind us?"

Devon smiled, "I did a year ago. Are you going to go in and see him?"

"I am," then glancing toward the outside door she added, "your friends are outside waiting for you."

Devon smiled at his mother, "We'll talk some more, let me go see what's going on out there."

The Parkers were standing in the street with Marshal Vaughn when Devon came out the door. Vaughn watched him come out and walk up to them. I've asked that a prison wagon be sent to haul them back in. I'm going to talk to Israel and Pat about keeping guard on them somewhere until it comes."

"You're not staying around then, Marshal?"

"I'd like to, but I've got a prisoner back home that I'm anxious to deal with."

Devon laughed, "I'll bet you are."

Vaughn then turned to Hack, "That was some tracking you did there son, to follow a trail for over seventy miles takes a man with some skill."

Hack shrugged, "It ain't all that hard."

"You know Hack, we need another Deputy Marshal to replace Dinton and I happen to have some pull with the head man. Ever think about being a lawman?"

Hack's eyes opened wide, "Me?"

"You've got what it takes son; you've got guts and a good head. I could teach you everything you need to know."

Hack's face reflected his wrestling with the idea. "I ... I never thought of such a thing before." He glanced over at his brother, "But I have to run the ranch with my brother."

Trig's eyes were dancing with amusement and he was wearing his customary grin.

Hack looked hard at him, "What are you laughin' at?"

"I'm not laughin' at you; I was just picturing a Parker with a badge."

"Is that bad?"

Abby came in between them. "No Hack, it's not bad. Have you boys heard about Judge Isaac Parker over in Fort Smith?"

Trig and Hack both acknowledged that they had.

"He's kin to us." Then looking at Trig she gave him a disapproving frown, "So a Parker with the law *ain't* so unusual."

Holding his hands out in a defensive position Trig laughed, "I never said it was bad, only that after the old man and all it's hard to picture a Parker with a badge ... but I'd like to."

Hack stared dumbfounded at his brother, "You would?"

"You bet, it's time we brought some respectability back to the Parker name."

Hack continued to stare at his brother and then turned his head toward the Marshal.

Trig broke back in, "You'd better get goin' little brother. The Marshal needs a good man to take care these outlaws ... and I can't think of a better man. Besides there's a lot of years to catch up on to clear the Parker name and make it a good name again. So, you'd best get to it."

Hack chuckled and shook his head, "Well, Marshal, you've got yourself a new man."

Vaughn smiled at him, "And proud to have you, too."

Trig then slapped his brother on the back, "Do us proud little brother."

The group watched as Hack and Marshal Vaughn walked away, headed toward the pens where Dodd and Lyons held the outlaws. Abby turned to Trig, "You boys started righting the Parker name the day you took up with us and picked the right side in the fight."

"Yeah, I guess we did. Now you go on in and see to Brian, I'm going to see if they need some help with Sloan's bunch."

Abby, Katy, and Devon turned and went back into the house. The door to Richards' room was open inviting them to come in. Stepping through the door Devon was surprised to see his mother sitting next to Richards' bed. He was awake and smiling, and it was apparent that they had been talking.

Marie turned her head and smiled, "Devon, did you know that Brian likes Longfellow?"

Devon smiled back at her, "No, but I'll bet you're going to read him some."

Katy elbowed him in the ribs, "Let's go. I think Brian is going to make a very quick recovery."

Devon laughed, "I wouldn't be surprised."

About the Author

Dave P. Fisher

Mountain men, Voyageurs, pioneers and explorers make up Dave's family tree. His mother's side was from Canada where men plied the fur trade. Some ventured into the Rocky Mountains during the beaver boom in the 1820's. Others moved into the wilds of Northern Minnesota and established trading posts among the Chippewa Indians.

On his father's side were soldiers, veterans of the War of 1812 and the Spanish American War. His natural grandfather died in the west while working as a railroad telegrapher. His step grandfather, born in the 1800's, was a Blackfoot Indian from Montana. He was a hunter and horseman who brought a great deal of Old West influence into the Fisher family.

Dave inherited that pioneer blood and followed in the footsteps of his ancestors. Originally from Oregon, he worked cattle and rode saddle broncs in rodeos. His adventures have taken him across the wilds of Alaska as a horsepacker and hunting guide, through the Rocky Mountains of Montana, Wyoming and Colorado where he guided and packed for a variety of outfitters.

Dave weaves his adventures and experiences into his writing. His style draws readers into the story with realism as a result of personal knowledge of the west, its people and character. His novels, numerous short stories, nonfiction articles and cowboy poetry have been internationally published. He was awarded the Will Rogers Medallion Award for Outstanding Western Fiction and his short stories have won numerous Reader's Choice Awards. Dave's Poudre Canyon Saga, published by Bottom of the Hill Publishing, is garnering fans around the world. Dave also contributed a short story, The Double Deal, in Bottom of the Hill's 2010 publication entitled TRAILS WEST. A MAN FOR THE COUNTRY is the sequel to the 2011 publication of BITTER GRASS.

CPSIA information can be obtained at www.ICGtesting.com
Printed in the USA
BVOW05s2249160314

347760BV00008B/161/P

9 781612 034706